STRANGE MEETING

ALSO BY SUSAN HILL

GHOST STORIES

The Small Hand

The Woman in Black

Dolly

The Man in the Picture

The Travelling Bag and Other Ghostly Stories

NOVELS

Strange Meeting

In the Springtime of the Year

I'm the King of the Castle

SHORT STORIES

The Boy who Taught the Beekeeper to Read
and other Stories

CRIME NOVELS

The Various Haunts of Men

The Pure in Heart

The Risk of Darkness

The Vows of Silence

The Shadows in the Street

NON-FICTION

Howards End is on the Landing

Jacob's Room is Full of Books

STRANGE MEETING

SUSAN HILL

P

PROFILE BOOKS

This edition published in Great Britain in 2018 by
Profile Books Ltd
3 Holford Yard
Bevin Way
London
WC1X 9HD

First published in Great Britain by Hamish Hamilton 1971.
Reprinted with an afterword by Penguin Books 1989.

www.profilebooks.com

10 9 8 7 6 5 4 3 2 1

Typeset in Transitional by MacGuru Ltd
Printed and bound in Great Britain by Clays, St Ives plc

A CIP catalogue record for this book is available from the British Library.

ISBN 978 1 78816 068 1

For John and Myfanwy Piper

PART ONE

He was afraid to go to sleep. For three weeks, he had been afraid of going to sleep.

But then, because of some old, familiar sound or smell, suddenly recalled, in this room of his overlooking the rose garden, he recalled also the trick he had used as a child, to keep himself awake.

He wanted to stay awake.

In the hospital, it had been different. Because of the pain in his leg, and because he could not bear the noises of the ward at night, the sounds of hoarse breathing and death, and the crying of the Field-Gunner in the next bed, he had only wanted to sleep. He had asked them to give him something, had tried and failed to get whisky or rum. He had even tried to bribe Crawford.

Crawford …

He remembered Crawford's eyes, and his soft jowls,
folding inwards towards the small nose, and mouth and
chin. Crawford, standing at the foot of his bed. It had not
surprised him, their meeting there. Nothing like that was
surprising now. Though, at first, Crawford had been busy
with the Field-Gunner, had not come near Hilliard until
the following day. Then, as always, in the past, their pointless, mutual dislike.

'Hello, Hilliard. Got it through the calf, did you?'

'Thigh.'

'Left?'

'Yes.'

'Bullet?'

'No, shrapnel.'

Crawford nodded. The flesh over his cheeks was carefully razored. But there were dark smears beneath his eyes,
as though he, too, did not sleep.

'Good for a month back home, then. You always were a
clever devil, Hilliard.'

When they were boys, they had both been sent to a
dancing class, held on Saturdays at eleven, in the Methodist Hall.

'If you are going to do a thing, do it properly,' Constance
Hilliard had said. 'There is nothing to be ashamed of in
learning dancing.' He had not supposed that there was.
His sister went too. 'Dancing will be a great asset to you
later on, you will have me to thank for having taken you
to proper lessons. I like a young man who knows how to

dance.' For she hoped that he would cut as good a figure
as his father, would look so fine and be so accomplished,
at the Waltz and the Lancers.

Saturday mornings in the Methodist Hall, and the smell
of dust between the grain of the floorboards, the squeak
of chalk where the steps were marked out, and, over the
echoing piano, the voice of Miss Marchment.

'The Crawfords are taking their boy,' his mother had
said, though she scarcely knew the Crawfords. Hilliard was
three years younger.

He had not been embarrassed by the dancing class, only
disliked it because he was no good, had no rhythm, could
not convert her instructions into the right, patterned
movements of his own feet.

'You are to try, you are to stick to it. It will suddenly go
"click" one morning, everything will fall into place, and
then you will be like your father, you will be a beautiful
dancer.'

He knew that he would not, but he did not care, either,
only went each Saturday and was bored – and sat out, much
of the time, because Miss Marchment became impatient.

'You have no *control,* John Hilliard, no co-ordination.'

Around the Methodist Hall, fat hot-water pipes ran like
intestines, the lead-colour showing through in patches
where the paint had worn away. He sat on the pipes and
felt the secret movement of the water beneath him. They
were warm pipes, though they did not give much of their
warmth out to the hall. He sat, unworried, watching the
others, watching Crawford. Crawford was good at dancing.

They had scarcely spoken to one another, then or later, the edges of their lives scarcely overlapped. They went away to different Prep schools, a hundred miles apart. In the years that followed, they met sometimes, at other people's parties. Once, they passed in different punts, on the Backs at Cambridge.

But they had scarcely spoken to one another. There was only this dislike. Now, he saw that it had been because of something in Crawford's expression, a smugness about the loose, soft cheeks, and the smallness of nose and mouth. But he was worried, this time, that someone he scarcely knew should have been, throughout his life, so consistently disliked. There ought to be no time, now, for that, no place for it. He was being petty.

Since going to the front in April, he had found out so many things, came up against traits like this, which he could not accept. He had thought, before April, that he knew himself. He was wounded during the second week of the offensive, in July. Came home again. Was twenty-two, then. Knew everything. Nothing.

And there had been Crawford, in a white coat, standing at the foot of his hospital bed. A familiar face. He had joined up straight from medical school, that first August.

'Been out there long?'

'April.'

'And got yourself a Mighty in July. I said you were a clever devil, Hilliard.'

Why? What do you know about me? You know nothing. I dislike you, Crawford.

But why that, either? Bloody silly. Childish. They were not children now. Crawford was Crawford. He had done nothing. Only that there was still the smugness of face, the fold of the jowls, the slight smile, as though he remembered that he had been good at dancing.

Dancing …

On the third night, he had tried to bribe him.

'I'll pretend I didn't hear that, Hilliard.'

'Look …'

'Pack you off home on Wednesday. We need the beds, God knows. Nice casualty train, calm sea if you're lucky. Month in Hawton. You'll be all right.'

'Crawford …'

'How's your sister?'

'I *can't sleep.*'

No. Only see the pale, moving lights, hear the screens drawn, metal scissors dropped into enamel bowls, hear the Field-Gunner with the bandaged face, crying.

'Think yourself lucky you got off a bit early. It's no picnic now.'

'What?'

'You've seen what's coming in here, and there'll be more. Something's still boiling up. We hear things, you know.'

But have you been there, Crawford, have you been?

Well, does that matter? He has to be here, doesn't he, somebody has to be here when they bring in the Field-Gunner, blinded.

Non-Combatant Forces. Crawford.

He wanted to sleep, shut out the noises. Why had it

been so easy up there, to sleep on a firestep, on a table in a cellar, to fall asleep on horseback going up the road to Bapaume, to sleep through the noise of the guns? Not now.

'I've got to sleep.'

Crawford had gone away.

Yet now, in the room above the rose garden, he was trying the old trick of staying awake, keeping his head above the green-black water of nightmares. Outside, it was still, except, in the distance, the faint wash of the sea.

The trick was, to order yourself to be dead asleep by the time you counted ten, or twenty. Then, you couldn't do it, you stayed awake, for as long as you wanted. Ten. Fifteen. Twenty. 'Go to sleep!' Though perhaps, when he was a child, in this room, he had never, in fact, wanted it to be so very long, only wanted time enough to see the guests who were coming to dinner, or hear the owl begin to hoot in the trees at the bottom of the drive. Once, he stayed awake for the arrival of his mother's cousin, who was a missionary in Africa (and who had been, after all, an ordinary woman in a dull green dress, who had been nothing, seen from two floors above through the stairwell, who bore no traces of Africa).

Now, he wanted to stay awake. There was nothing to hear, for the owls had moved away some years ago, there were no visitors to see, he was no longer a child excluded from secrets. Now, there were no secrets. His leg was better, that would not keep him awake. It only ached slightly when he had been walking, or in the cold. But it was not cold, it was late August, it had been hot all the weeks at Hawton. Hot in France, too.

He had been unhappy at home, where he could talk to no one, nobody knew, where they gave dinner parties and agreed about politics, where old men aired their military opinions and he could not join in, only sit there, staring at them, and then down his food, in disbelief. He had argued twice, bitterly, with his father. But after that, stayed silent. He had gone to London and wandered hopelessly about the streets, eaten in the club and listened to what they were saying there, too, had seen that life went on: flower-sellers sitting around Piccadilly, young women with parasols strolling in the sunshine through Green Park, commissionaires in uniform, opening the doors of grand hotels. Uniform … He had felt a tightening in his head. Spoke to no one. Returned home. On the lawn under the cedar tree, his mother poured China tea for the ladies who came on Wednesdays to knit, grey and green socks and mittens and helmets, for the coming winter at the front. They turned their heads to watch him as he walked, limping slightly, up the gravelled path. The shadows were long and black, against the brightness of the sun. He had so hated being here.

But there? Would he rather be there again? Or even where Crawford was, far behind the front line, standing at the foot of beds, hundreds of beds. For it had gone on, grown worse, throughout that summer. Crawford had known what they all knew. 'We hear things.'

Although, in England you could not tell exactly what was

happening, only the official reports came through to the newspapers, telling nothing. He read them, read between the lines, read the Casualty Lists. Imagined. Knew.

Knew that he had been wrong, unfair to Crawford, that there was no place for such petty feelings now. Could he have stood it himself, night after night in the military hospital, hearing the terrible noises? He should not continue to dislike Crawford.

This was how it went on, he felt himself changing daily, felt himself to be old, twenty, thirty, fifty years older than when he had gone out in April. Hardened, too. He knew. Everything. There were no secrets. He scarcely recognized the person he had once been, the person his family seemed to remember.

He did not want to go to sleep. He ordered himself not to, and so it would work, the old, childhood trick. He turned his head on the pillow, keeping his eyes open.

It did not work, for he was conditioned, now, to obeying, not countermanding orders. Ten. Fifteen. Twenty. 'Go to sleep!' He slept.

But at first, he dreamed only of horses, standing beside a hawthorn hedge in winter. The dark twigs were laced over with frost. There were four or five horses, and the breath came out of their nostrils and rose to hang and freeze, whitening on the air. He heard the soft thud of hoof on hard earth and the metal bits champing. Their muzzles were like the soft backs of moles.

He half woke, turned over. Horses? The first time he had ridden a horse was out across the Wiltshire Downs from the Training Camp, early that year. He had written so, in a letter home:

I'm settling down quite well here. We're a mixed bunch but we get along. Some of it's far pleasanter than I'd expected. For instance, I'm riding a horse for the first time in my life, and enjoying it greatly.

His mother had written back at once:

You are quite wrong about the riding, John. When you were four you rode a donkey on the sands at Eastbourne. Indeed, there is a photograph of you somewhere, sitting on a donkey and looking pleased. You were wearing a blue sun-hat. So you have certainly ridden before.

He had thought of recounting it, as a funny story, to Mason-Godwin, who shared the hut with himself and Archer. But did not do so in the end, because it seemed disloyal, Mason-Godwin was not a friend. Was humourless. A neat man.

That was the first time he had wished for Beth, for he could have begun to tell his sister the story and she would have at once supplied the ending, laughed with him, knowing their mother.

He would like to see her. But he felt no nostalgia for Hawton, then or later, and had been ashamed of that at first. He was indifferent to home, to mother or father. He disliked neither of them, but did not particularly miss them. Nor had he any ties with friends or his own past. All around him, the men of B Company told stories, about mothers and wives and friendly neighbours, became sentimental towards evening, in the billets at Selcourt, sang. Hilliard read their letters for censoring and passed over the conventional phrases of love and longing with curious detachment. Though certainly he looked forward to getting the mail that came to him, as much as any of them did, looked forward to his mother's parcels, and the letters full of moral encouragement, and local gossip. Anything that broke the monotony, or the fear.

But he missed his sister. Beth's letters were rather formal, disappointing. Communication between them had never been stated, they had relied upon thoughts and moments of humour, taken one another for granted. Were shocked by separation. The letters said nothing.

For a while, half-sleeping again, he still heard the gentle tossing of the horses' heads, saw their breath smoking, saw ice meshed with cracks across a puddle.

Outside in the darkness, a hundred yards away, the soil became paler and drier, became sand, and the path led down to the beach.

His leg cramped suddenly, jerking him awake, but then at once he fell heavily asleep again, a hand came over his face, thick, moist and cold as an ether mask, and forced him down into the nightmares.

By day, walking about the garden or along the beaches in the hot sun, he had tried to remember the tiredness of the trenches, the lack of sleep that tipped him over into

hysteria, to remember the longing for a mattress, sheets, a
feather pillow. And there they were, on his own bed, in his
own room. For three and a half weeks, he had been trying
not to sleep.

The nightmares rose up through him in waves, like
bouts of nausea, and at their crest, burst open and spilled
over one another in confusion. Tomorrow, he was travelling to rejoin the battalion.

As he came awake the second time, he heard himself
cry out. Had anyone else heard him? He sat up quickly, to
shut out the sound of his own heart, thumping against the
pillows, the rush of blood through his ears.

The day they had taken the German trench, they found
the bodies piled on top of one another in layers, like sandbags, making a wall.

Jesus God, help me …

It was very quiet in his room. He moved his arm over the
mound of quilt and blanket, and the memory came back to
him of the soft bodies. And then, the soft bolsters through
which he had had to thrust a bayonet every morning that
spring. Bayonet practice had been the only thing he could
not take, at the Training Camp. He hated the look of the
blade, and the click as you fixed it home, the idea that it
was somehow an extension of his own arm. Rifle shooting
had been different, a skill to master and almost a matter of
pride, to aim through the pale, clear light of March, across
the open field to a neat target. He found that he was rather
good at shooting. But not the bayonet.

The sweat was cooling on his back. The worst thing

in his nightmares was always the smell, the sweet, rotten trench smell, of soil and chlorine and blood, and the mustard gas like garlic. His bedroom window was open and the room was full of the scent of roses, coming up from the warm garden. A sweet smell, and curiously like some cream or powder in a jar on his mother's dressing table. A sweet smell.

He pushed the bedclothes away, retching, leaned over the washbasin and felt the walls of his stomach clench uselessly. Only a little water came up into his mouth, tasting bitter. He ran the tap and rinsed his mouth out, splashed his face. Shivered. Yet he had never been sick in France, not even felt sick, and only once had he had to turn his face away at the sight of a wound. He did not retch at the real things, only the memory of them, here in his old room above the rose garden.

Tomorrow, he was going back, and he would rather that than go back now to his bed. He had to get out of this room. He could still smell the roses.

It was somehow reassuring just to be putting on his clothes, to feel cotton and Shetland wool against his skin. He went out, walking on the grass in case the crunch of his feet on the drive woke them, and his mother should call out or come down, urging him back to bed, to sleep.

He went between the fruit trees into the copse, and took the path leading down to the beach. It was very warm, the sky clear and pricked all over with stars. First he heard the soft hiss and suck of the sea, and then saw it, thin and silvered as a snail's trail where the moon lay along its edge.

The tide was right out, so that he had to wade through mounds of loose sand before it became damp, firm and satisfying under the soles of his feet. It was a wide bay, curved between two wooded tongues of land, and the coast continued like this, open and gentle, for more than twenty miles, before the cliffs grew steeper and more rocky, the currents dangerous. He lit a cigarette and the striking of the match, on open ground at night, made him panic, turn and look behind him, before he remembered where he was. He threw the match into a pool between two ribs of sand. Then, he began to walk slowly along the water line, no longer afraid, but poised between a sense of reassurance, at the sound of the night sea, and despair, because he had been at home and unhappy for three and a half weeks, he cared nothing for any of them, could explain nothing. He was simply waiting. For?

His mind filled up suddenly with ordinary details, about his journey back tomorrow, about what he should not forget to take with him, things he had promised people – a bottle of old brandy, chocolate, a good torch, a pair of wire cutters that would actually cut wire, Gilbert and Sullivan music for Reevely, who sang so badly and had such ambitions: he wondered where he would find his battalion, where they would be going to next, who was left. He thought – I want to go back. For there was nothing for him here.

'You must go across to The White Lodge,' Constance Hilliard had said, during the first week of his leave. 'The Major is so anxious for you to go and have a talk to him, he feels so out of things. He doesn't see so well nowadays.

You must be very patient with him. I have told him that you will be coming.'

Up the short, ill-kempt drive, then, past the kennel where the bulldog lay as it had always lain, and snarled at him and snuffled up its thick nose, an evil dog, smelly, old, fat. Up to the blue door.

'He has always taken an interest in you, always. He used to give you sweets when you were only a toddler. You won't remember that.' He remembered.

'He is looking forward to a long talk with you.'

The Major who had only daughters, five daughters, one of whom was left to keep house so inefficiently, and attend Constance Hilliard's knitting parties. She smelled, too, as the bulldog smelled and the dim hallway and the Major's own study. An old smell, faintly rancid.

What would he find to say to the Major?

'Pity you weren't a cavalryman.'

'Oh, I'm happy where I am, on the whole.'

'Pity.'

'I do ride. We have horse transport.'

'You should have been a cavalryman, you've got a good long leg. Far and away the most useful, cavalry, always were. You're only clearing a way for them now, of course, you do realize that?'

Clearing a way.

'Pity you're not a cavalryman. Still … Come with me while I feed the dog. I always feed the dog about now. What time is it, exactly? Still, you'll be back again before Christmas, before the year's out. Yes. All be over. Hold that dish steady. I have to cut the meat up a bit, he hasn't the teeth he once did, have to help him on. Come with me. Look here, you've no cause to hang behind, he's harmless isn't he? Look … You remember him well enough, don't you, you used to come here from school a year or so ago – he's harmless.'

The dog heaved on to its legs and strained at the chain. Hilliard stood back from the smell of its body, as it sweated in the autumn sun.

'Given you long enough at home with your feet up though, haven't they? You seem to be all right. Don't mind the dog. He takes his time, he isn't so good managing his food as he used to be. Likes me to stand with him, you see. Had you no ambition to go for the cavalry?'

The Major had offered him tea, and when it came, into the close-windowed study, he had only been able to drink, though the Major ate hugely, chicken and tongue sandwiches, currant loaf, eclairs, slapping the food noisily about his mouth. Hilliard looked out of the window. The White Lodge was a pink bungalow, in need of repainting. Thistles and dock had seeded themselves among the currant bushes of the garden.

'Seen anything of the Russians?'

'I've been in France.'

'No, no.' The eclair oozed cream over his fingers and he sucked them. 'No, *Russians*. Don't you read your papers, keep up to date? They're here, the country's full of them. Well, ask Kemble down at the station, he sees the trains go through at night, troop trains full of them, he'll tell you. I thought you'd know all about it.'

'Would you mind if I opened the window?'

'I get rheumatism. It's the damp. The dog gets it too, come to that. I get bronchitis in the winter.'

The window stayed shut. Over the top of the hedge, straggling with convolvulus, Hilliard saw the thin gold line of the sea, and the heat shimmering in between.

'Cavalrymen always were more highly thought of.'

When he left, he took in great gulps of air, but it was not fresh, even outside, it was dusty, old, burned-up air, the end of summer. The dog heaved, growling deep inside its massive belly.

'You'll be back here before Christmas. They know what they're doing.'

He stood at the broken gate, unable to see Hilliard beyond the first few yards of the road.

'The Major always asks after you, John. He was a fine soldier in his day. He takes an interest in you, a pride, even. He didn't have a boy of his own. It's a pity he doesn't see so well now. He isn't old, you know, not so very old. He feels left out of things. It's a great pity.'

Half a mile on, he came to a small cluster of rocks, and sat down. He did not notice that they were damp, from the seaweed trailing over them, he was so used, now, to physical discomforts. The first night they arrived at the Training Camp, they had slept in a field because there was confusion over hut accommodation, too many officers sent to this one place. They had a groundsheet and one army blanket each. It was early March, bitterly cold. In the morning, they rose like shadows, scarcely able to see one another at ten yards distance, through a thick mist. The grass was soaking wet, their blankets and valises and the overcoats in which most of them had slept were wet. All the admonitions of childhood had come back to him, about damp feet and the perils of fog to the lungs, he had waited for pleurisy, bronchitis, pneumonia. He did not even catch cold, and had not been ill once, the whole time there, or in France, had felt, indeed, more than usually well, with an odd lightheadedness. The shrapnel wound in his thigh had healed very quickly.

The sea moved about, turning over and back upon itself at the shore line. Then, he thought that he could hear, even from so far away, the thudding of the guns. But there were so many noises now, imagined or remembered, filling his head as he walked about the lanes and fields beyond Hawton that summer, he could no longer trust his own judgement.

He thought, I want to go back. In the pit of his stomach, a flutter of apprehension, excitement.

He reached down and let his hand touch the water in a rock pool. It was quite warm and glimmering from some faint phosphorescence and then, as it stirred, the briny smell came up into his nostrils, reminding him of all the summers of his childhood. There were limpets, rough and conical, clinging to the sides of the pool, and he rubbed over them with the pads of his fingers. Immediately, he was conscious of his own flesh, of the nerves beneath the skin, of the bone and muscle which obeyed him: clench, unclench, move this finger, bend that. His hands looked huge and pale under the water. He had never realized before how much he cared about his own body, simply because it was so familiar, because he knew better than he knew anything every shape and crease of it, the exact width of knuckle, the flatness of his fingernails. So that, when he imagined his hand torn off at the wrist it was not the thought of the pain which so terrified him, but simply the loss of a part of himself, something he had always known. He *was* his hand and his legs and neck, ribs and groin. Yet the wound had healed well enough.

He tried to pull a limpet away and felt it sucking in hard, resisting him. He knew that in the end he would win, could prise under the shell and probe out the weak spot in its defences. For a second he rested his fingers on the ribbed surface. Then let go abruptly, ashamed. He got up and began to walk back, looking down at the pebbles that glistened, dark as glass, where the water touched them. The easy movement of his own long legs pleased him, he could have walked on for mile after mile, for ever.

Going up the road from Bapaume that Saturday afternoon, after eleven days in the front line without relief, Hurstfield, one of his own platoon, had swayed, staggered and then fallen, and the others had hauled him up and marched him between them for a while, supporting his arms, telling him to move his feet, left right, left right, left right, so that he obeyed them, like a drunk being taken home. They had been marching since seven, had passed the far point of exhaustion, rested for a quarter of an hour, gone on, and in the end, Hurstfield seemed to get strength again, he shook off their hands and moved away a little from them. Roberts the Welshman had taken over some of his pack but now, seeing the look on Hurstfield's face, handed it back to him without speaking. Hilliard watched tensely, riding alongside them until a message came up for him to go ahead and meet the Adjutant at the crossroads. He forgot about Hurstfield. He was tired himself, his head ached in the sun. But the men were walking.

As he came off the beach he heard it again, the distant boom, like an explosion at the end of a long tunnel. An owl hooted. So they had come back then.

Owls, ravens, hedgehogs, snakes – augurs of death and mischance. But he had seen none of them in Picardy. Only lizards basking on their bellies against hot stone walls, only flocks of magpies and larks, soaring up out of sight at the end of the day, only hard black beetles and, in the copse at Selcourt, a nightingale. He had gone for a walk along the canal bank and watched a kingfisher dive down to a fish.

Yet until this year, he had scarcely known the name of any tree, though there was countryside all around Hawton, he took no interest in the garden, perhaps because of his father's obsession with it, certainly had never been able to distinguish one bird from another. The owls had only pleased him because, as a child, he had found an odd comfort in their nightly hooting, and because of the tiny bones of the animals they hunted and ate, and which he used to pick out of their pellets. An owl could swallow a fieldmouse whole, and still digest it. He washed the bones and saved them, they might be somewhere in a drawer, still, for his mother allowed nothing to be thrown away.

Cliff House stood back, long and low and pale in the moonlight. Around it, the lawns, about whose closeness of cut his father worried the gardener daily, the symmetrical flowerbeds, the perfectly pruned roses. He had been born here. The windows were tall and blank. It meant nothing to him. He felt a quiet misery, that he had somehow failed, because of that. Tomorrow he was rejoining his battalion. Did he not even mind, then, that he might never see this house again?

His head sang. Jesus God, *help me* …

Beth. Beth. He had always gone to Beth. He began to run.

For some reason, after having learned to swim early and well, he had for a short time become afraid of the water. He had said nothing about this, only not gone out very far, paddled about at the edges where his feet could keep in contact with the sand. It was the beginning of the holidays. Beth had watched him. She had never liked swimming.

'Come on.'

'What?'

'Come on. I want you to come out with me. I want to swim as far as the headland and back.' She had spoken very quickly, bobbing up and down like a cork in the water beside him. 'Come with me.'

'You don't like it,' John had said.

'I want to go.' Her face went blank, stubborn, so that she looked like their father. She wanted to help him.

In the end, he said, 'It's not too far.' But he was doubtful.

'I know it's not, don't I?'

They waited, swam a little way, only just out of their depth. The sea was milky green. If they went a little further, they would be able to see Cliff House, up on the slope behind the trees.

'I want to *go.*' And she had gone, pushing ahead of him in a slow breast-stroke, the movements of her arms very careful, so that he knew she was counting, as she had been taught. She had been far more afraid than he was.

'Here I come! Here I come!' He had swum hard and fast, not allowing himself to stop or think, and then they were side by side, out as far as the end of the headland, they could survey the whole of the bay, lying on their backs and floating on the soft mattress of the sea.

'I can see the windmill.'

'I can see the house.'

'I can see father. He's in a deckchair.'

'He's wearing his panama hat.'

'He's gone to sleep.'

'I can see your bedroom window. It's open.'

'I can see the whole, whole world.'

'I can see a bird on a currant bush. And it's a sparrow. I can see its *eyes.*'

'Liar!'

'I can so!'

He dived down and opened his eyes under the water, looking into darker and darker blue-greenness.

'John … John …' Her voice came from very far away, sounding different, hollow. 'John …'

He surfaced, bubbling. 'It's all right, stupid.'

'You could drown. You shouldn't do it.'

'There might be a shipwreck under here. I might go down and see.'

'Don't, you're not to … Oh, *don't* …' Her voice rose in anxiety.

He had laughed, circled her once, and then begun to make for the shore, knowing that she had had enough, and was even doubting if she could get back, though would not say so. She followed him at her own cautious pace. When they finally came up on to the beach she was breathing quickly, but she had raced before him up the path, said nothing about any of it. He had never again been afraid of swimming. Beth was older than him, by eighteen months, she had been almost eleven then. Beth. Beth …

He began to pant, climbing the stairs through the dark house, his hands were trembling. He tried not to count over all the possible ways in which, after tomorrow, he was going to die. Beth. Beth.

'BETH!'

She sat bolt upright in her bed, eyes huge and shocked out of sleep.

'I wondered what on earth it was! You frightened me.'

Had she forgotten all the times in the past when he had come here like this, for comfort, in the middle of the night? He sat on her bed, still trying to get his breath, wiping a hand over his face.

'Is it your leg? Is it hurting?'

He shook his head.

Beth's room was on the other side of the house, away from the terrible scent of the roses. She had pulled on her blue dressing gown and, when he looked at her, and saw the thick brown hair, which she wore carefully piled up during the day, falling on to her shoulders, she seemed to be younger, the same Beth.

They had not put the light on.

'You're dressed?'

'I went out. I've been on to the beach.'

'What on earth for? It's three o'clock.'

'Twenty past three.'

'Was it your leg?'

'I walked a long way. The tide's right out. It's been so quiet down there.' He spoke very slowly, pausing for a long time in between phrases.

'Beth …'

He had not told any of them about the nightmares, but sometimes at breakfast he had seen Beth looking at him and thought that he did not have to tell her, that she knew, as she had always known everything about him.

In her youth, Constance Hilliard had been a great beauty, and she was beautiful still. But Beth had inherited their father's long bony face, the high, narrow bridge to a nose that, in age, would become beak-like. Her hair grew far back from a very high forehead. Only her eyes, flint-coloured and thickly lashed, made her seem beautiful sometimes, because of their stillness.

He said, 'You're twenty-three, Beth.' It amazed him.

'Almost twenty-four.'

They sat in silence again, and he thought, then, of all the things that he wanted to tell her, which she did not know after all, had not guessed: the dread of returning to sleep, the faces of men in his nightmares, the voices, the sweet smell. Beth looked stern and, in spite of her hair falling about her face, looked her age, or even older, a woman. So she, too, had changed, though until tonight he had not fully realized it. This was another reason why the weeks at Hawton had not been happy. He had expected to spend time with her, walking about the beach, to laugh with her, explain things, but she had been busy, going out to lunch with their mother, helping twice a week at parties for soldiers on leave, leading a social life.

Hilliard had been to one of the parties, at which men sat along trestle tables lined down the church hall, and ate jellies and egg sandwiches and small, dainty cakes, their faces shocked and pale from the recollection of horrors. They had their photographs taken, looking embarrassed, and the women who served them, women like his mother and Beth and the wife of the Rector, stood by, looking proud and pleased. What do you think you are doing, he had wanted to say, what good is this? What good is this? But they were doing what seemed to them best, they knew nothing better, who was he to tell them the truth?

'Your leg *is* better, isn't it? They have said you're really all right to go back?'

'Oh, for God's sake, it's not my leg, my leg's nothing. Why do you go on and on about my leg?'

'Don't shout so, you'll wake mother. I was only wanting to know.'

'You look so *prim* now.'

At once, her face took on a stubborn cast, but then, as though she were consciously making an effort for him, softened.

'Are you afraid to go back?'

He stared at her. She had had to ask him that. She was like all the others, understood nothing.

'No,' he said.

'Perhaps it'll be all right now. You've had your wound, so you're not due for another.' He thought that she believed it.

'I don't think it works like that.'

'Oh, well … It's been lovely having you at home.'

He thought she sounded like a hostess speaking to a departing guest.

On the chest of drawers across the room was a small leather photograph frame, standing open. He saw himself, looking foolish and pale and ethereal in his uniform cap. The edges of the picture had been somehow blurred out and made to look cloudy, his eyes were glistening. It had been taken the day before he left for the Training Camp. It was some stranger.

Beth shifted a little in her bed, fidgeted with the quilt, as though she might want to say something, or else to be left to go back to sleep. But the sound reminded him of the nights he had crept into this room and under her bed and gone to sleep there, on the rose-patterned carpet in the stuffy dark, with the hanging fringe of the coverlet, which was like the blankets over the door of the dugout. The creak of the springs as his sister moved was like the sound of the man sleeping above him in the wire-framed bunk.

He had always been forbidden to sleep in his sister's room. In the mornings she had woken first and, knowing that he was there, leaned down and lifted the cover, whispering to him to go back quickly. He saw her face upside down, hair hanging. Outside, the sound of the martins and swifts that nested in the eaves of Cliff House. He had not minded returning to his room then.

That had gone on for what seemed like most of his childhood, but could only have been perhaps two summers when he was three or four years old. If he could creep under her bed now and lie on his back on the pink-flowered carpet, he would be able to sleep, he would be entirely safe, the nightmares would not come. In the dugout, there were soft voices behind the grey blankets passing messages, warning about careless lights or noises, sudden footsteps stopping abruptly: and the odd silences between, as when a train stopped in the middle of the countryside, and went still, so that through the windows came the calling of birds.

He felt calmer now, his head clear. Perhaps it was over, and he would simply sleep. Beth was watching him. He smiled at her, and she did not smile back. She said, 'There's a secret. But I think I could tell you now you're going back.' Her voice was cool, formal as the letters. 'I may marry Henry Partington.'

Then he knew that his sister had gone completely from him.

'John?'

For a moment she looked concerned, wanting his approval.

Henry Partington, a lawyer who played golf with their father, who had looked as he looked now for as long as Hilliard could remember, though he must be only forty-five or -six, who had a son, was long widowed, had been to dinner twice in the past three weeks and talked the way they were all talking here. But Hilliard had not guessed, had seen nothing. How could he have seen? *Henry Partington*.

'He's a very good man. He's so kind. I've really grown quite fond of him.'

He tried to take in what she was saying but could not do so, even in the light of the realization that his sister had changed, had altogether gone away from him. Until, suddenly, it became clear. For who else was there for her? They were all away, her old friends, all being killed, there were no prospects. Beth was not beautiful, she was almost twenty-four, and had their father and mother to contend with daily.

He stood up.

'John – I'm sorry I didn't tell you but … but I haven't actually said anything to him yet, I haven't …'

'You will.'

'He thinks very highly of you, John. I've often talked to him about you.'

How? What had there been to say? She knew nothing about him now.

'You're not offended are you? Because I didn't tell you?'

His hand rested on the cold china of the door knob. Tomorrow, he was going back, it was all right, nothing else could touch him.

He said, 'Of course not. You've every right to your own secrets.'

'Not a secret, but … Oh, you know.'

'Yes.'

She was still sitting up, hugging her arms around her knees. If he came home again, this room would be empty. He tried to picture her in a wide bed with Henry Partington, and because she was no longer the same person for him, it was easy, it seemed entirely fitting.

He said, 'It's a good idea. I think you will be perfectly happy.'

'Oh, John! Yes, you're right, I will, I know I will. But I did want you to see it, I did want you to think so.'

He smiled, turned the door handle.

'John – why did you go on to the beach? Was anything the matter?' She had lowered her voice again, the old conspiracy, not to waken their parents.

'Is it because you don't want to go back tomorrow?'

'No.'

He went back to his room and closed the window, to shut out the scent of the roses, he lay on the top of his bed, fully dressed, waiting for the first, thin light of morning.

His mother said, 'I shall come with you to the station.'

'NO!' But seeing her face, he added more quietly, 'I think I should prefer to go alone.'

For the truth was that he was leaving early, far too early. He could have caught an afternoon train from Hawton, for he did not have to embark until late that night, which should mean – even allowing for the crowds and the delays and the slowness of travel – not leaving Victoria until evening. But he had been up by seven with everything packed and ready. His room seemed once again as if it no longer belonged to him, the bed stripped, the top of the dressing table empty. He had looked into all the cupboards and drawers, and seen the things his mother had stored away – his school books and the shirts and trousers and socks he wore when he was twelve, the Meccano, the shells and stones he used to collect, cricket photographs: and, in one of his father's old tobacco tins, the small, bleached bones from the owls' pellets.

He wanted to be on his way.

'I didn't mean to come to London, John. But I would just like to walk with you down to the village, to see you on to the train.'

They were standing far apart from one another in the morning room. Constance Hilliard had her back to him, was looking out through the tall windows on to the lawn, baked and yellowing after the long weeks of summer. His father was becoming obsessive about the state of the lawns, pacing about them each morning and evening, poking with his stick, and holding, bitter, repetitive conversations with Plummet.

Once, his mother's hair had been butter-coloured, but he could scarcely remember that, she had gone grey very

early. Now, the sun made it glint with a curiously artifi-
cial light, like something concocted out of wire and floss
by a theatrical wigmaker. She was a tall woman, tightly
corseted, upright. But not graceful, though she always
wore graceful clothes, which flowed and folded about her,
she was fondest of silks and cashmere and lawn. Her dress
today was of lawn, pale cream, with full sleeves and a high
neck, bands of lace.

'You look as if you were going to a wedding, mother.'
Though in truth she might always have been dressed for
some wedding – or garden party or dinner or opera, she
was a provincial woman who bought the type of clothes
designed for some London society hostess. She said, 'I do
have standards.' As a boy he had been embarrassed by the
grandeur of her costume, when she came to see him at
school. They said, 'Who is she? Who is she?'

'Hilliard's mother.'

'Only Hilliard? Good Lord!'

The sun shone, too, on the round walnut table which
stood between them, on the Meissen figurine, and the
copy of *Blackwood's* and the bowl of roses. Roses.

'I am dressed to come with you to the railway station.'

He was silent for a moment. Somewhere, around the
side of the house, Plummet began to mow the lawn.

'Look, actually I do have to go fairly soon, mother. I've
got some things to do in London … shopping … and …'

'You won't be staying for luncheon?'

'I-no. I'd better be off.'

'Is there anything you like to have in your parcels?

Anything in particular? It is so awfully difficult to know. Your father was asking.'

'Whatever you like. Anything, thank you.'

'Fruit? Sweets?'

'Yes.'

'You used to be fond of muscatels and almonds, as a small boy. Mary will bake you plum cakes, of course, they are so much better than anything we could buy.'

'I don't mind what you send, mother. Anything.'

'Fortnum's are very reliable, I think? You do get what we ask for? They send out things of good quality?'

'Yes, yes.'

'Now you are to complain, John, if anything is not quite right. We pay enough for the parcels, they should not put in substitutes, or anything which is not of the best.'

'Mother, the parcels are perfectly all right, don't go on about things. I'm grateful for whatever you send, that's all. Don't *trouble*.'

'I like to trouble. That is the least I can do.'

He did not reply. Looking at his mother then, she seemed less of a stranger than she had ever been, almost closer, now, than Beth. He could hardly believe it. She had not changed, she looked no older. There had been no real communication between them since he came home, no more than throughout his life. Yet for this time, he loved her.

He knew little enough about her, however, did not even know tiny, factual things – as, what particular illnesses she had suffered in childhood, where she had first met his father, what she did in the mornings after breakfast, when she shut herself up in her sitting room overlooking the bay and would not see anyone, how much money she had to spend.

Her hands were folded together, palm to palm, in front of her. What kind of a woman? Would he be able to say anything at all about her when he got back to France?

From the bowl on the table in front of him came the terrible scent of roses.

'I had better go. I really ought to leave quite soon.'

'Is there a great deal you have to carry?'

'Oh, no. Anyway, I've got used to lugging things about.'

'Then perhaps we might walk. As it's such a fine morning. As you are going before it gets too hot. Perhaps we could walk to the railway station?'

No, he thought, no. He wanted to leave Cliff House alone, to turn the bend by the blackthorn hedge and go out of their sight, he wanted to go.

He said, 'All right, mother. If you feel like it. I'll get my bags downstairs.'

Constance Hilliard nodded. And went to get ready also, to put on a huge, cream-coloured hat and pin it with pearl-headed pins, to change her shoes and take up the lace parasol, to look like a Queen, walking down the grav-elled drive and along the lane and up to the main street of Hawton towards the station.

They said nothing. He saw that people looked at her, and he was no longer embarrassed by her extravagance of dress and her height and her coolness of manner, for he understood, suddenly, that she was obliged to make the best of what she had, here in this dull, restricted neighbourhood, and that she was perhaps unhappy, after all, bored with herself. He saw that she was beautiful.

By the time they reached the station he was sweating inside the heavy uniform, his shirt collar felt tight as iron. It was only a little after ten-thirty and already the sun was high and hot in a silvery sky. The awnings of the ticket office and the waiting room cast hard-edged shadows. On the opposite platform a young woman sat, nursing a child. Nobody else. They walked a little way up, beyond the buildings, towards a bench.

'Off back then,' Kemble said – Kemble who had seen the phantom Russian troop trains go through Hawton like thieves in the night, Kemble who remembered all the times he had waited here for a train to go back to school.

'Kemble is letting this station go,' Constance Hilliard said firmly, looking about her at the banks on either side of the line, where the grass grew tall and was seeding itself, with poppies and sorrel in between.

'It always used to be so neat and tidy, we used to be proud of our station, but he seems not to care as he did. His son was killed at Mons. Do you remember Kemble's boy? Or else he is too old, it has got too much for him.'

And it was true that the paint was flaking off the name sign, there were cracks in the green bench, a few sweet papers and cigarette packets lay as they had been dropped, in corners, to gather the summer's dust.

'Perhaps they don't let him have any money for refurbishments.'

'It isn't a question of money. He could take a *pride* in things.' She poked at a dandelion, growing up through a crevice in the stone, at her feet. 'He has let everything go.'

She looked as if she would never let go, would never allow herself to loosen her corset, to have a crease in a dress or a spot of dirt left on her glove. She did not stand still beside him but walked up and down in the sunlight, casting a long, rippling shadow. She might have been nervous. Hilliard saw the young woman with the child watching her, saw Kemble the station master watching her. As he himself watched her. Was she aware of it?

It was very quiet. A pair of cabbage-white butterflies fluttered up and down like tiny kites blown by some breeze. But there was no breeze, no movement of air at all. Sun. Heat. Country silence. The rustle of his mother's dress as she turned towards him again.

He thought, she has told me that Kemble's son was killed, at Mons, and has gone on to speak of other things. Does she not know? Does she not think of it?

She said, 'We look forward to your letters.'

Her skin was hardly lined, it had the moist look of chamois, though there was a tightness about the eyes and throat which revealed her age. He wondered if Beth felt bitter that she did not inherit such beauty, as he did. For he had his mother's features, though they were arranged less disdainfully, he had the same grey eyes and pale hair and length of limb.

He looked at the gloved hand holding the parasol, at the small, flat ears beneath her hat. Should he say something to her? What would be the truth?

'I shall not worry over you. I promised myself that when you first went away. Your father says that you will all be home by Christmas, in any case, it will be all over. And there is really no point in one's worrying or one would simply never stop.'

'Oh, no. Quite.'

'There are so many things one could begin to imagine.'

Could they?

'So many things are possible.'

Yes.

'So you see, one simply tells oneself not to worry.'

Kemble had come out of his office holding the flag. Across the metals of the rails, the heat shimmered. The girl with the child had not moved, was still watching Constance Hilliard. Nobody else had come. He knew that when he left here he would not be able to believe it would all continue to exist, would go on in the same way, no matter where he himself was, or what happened to him. A small station, ill-kempt, with a ridiculously large clock. Butterflies. Long grass and sorrel. Half a mile away, the sea. Hawton.

'Really, John, it's quite like you're going off to school, only then there always seemed to be more of a rush and a fuss, you never organized yourself in those days, you always chased about the house and forgot things and made us late. You haven't forgotten anything today?'

'I don't think so.'

He knew that he had not, that there was nothing left of himself at Cliff House, only pieces of a past belonging to some stranger. Everything he had, everything he was, stood on this quiet platform in the sunlight, a tall young man in uniform, who had seen what he had seen, who knew – some belongings packed into a dark valise. Nothing more.

In the distance, the train was coming, very slowly, leaving behind a trail of steam, each puff of which remained separate upon the air.

'Really, I think I shall have to ask Mr Kemble to ring up for Plummet, it is getting altogether too hot to walk back to Cliff House. I have to lunch with the Callenders and I do so hate getting dusty. But I should get dusty. I should have to change again. Perhaps I am dusty already?'

'No, mother.'

For she was not. When the train pulled out, he looked back for a long time and saw her tall figure in the huge hat and the cream-coloured skirts, standing motionless in the sun. They did not wave to one another. On the opposite platform the girl sat, holding the child, transfixed by the sight of Constance Hilliard. And the picture of the two of them like that remained in his mind and was thrown up by it every so often, without reason, during the weeks and months that followed, like some painting remembered from a gallery. There were moments when he forgot that it had not, in fact, been a painting, had been real.

The train was almost empty. He put his case up on the rack and unbuttoned his tunic and dozed, watching the parched fields and thick, lustreless trees glide by the window, thinking of nothing, neither past nor future. He had, again, the odd sense of completeness, of holding everything within himself, of detachment.

It was the thirtieth of August.

By three o'clock in the afternoon there was nothing left for him to do. He had been to The Army and Navy Stores and gone slowly from counter to counter buying what he needed, and after that, looking, looking. The war had brought out a fever like that of Christmas among manufacturers and salesmen, there were so many possible things to buy, expressly for the men in France. Hilliard watched people buying them, mothers, aunts, sisters, wives, who had no idea what might be really suitable, who wanted to send something extra, who were misled by the advertisements and the counter staff into ordering useless gifts to be packed up and sent. He saw bullet-proof waistcoats and fingered them in amazement, remembering the bullets, saw leather gauntlets, too stiff and thick and hot, saw ornamental swords and pistols of use only to gamekeepers, saw the shining new metal of entrenching tools and spurs.

But he wanted to buy something then, something that was entirely superfluous, an extravagance, a gift to himself. He moved about among the women and could see nothing, felt as he had felt on a day's outing from school, when the money his father had given him burned a hole in his pocket and he was almost in tears at the frustration of finding nothing he desired to buy.

He spent more than two pounds on a pale cane walking-stick with a round silver knob, and, carrying it out into the sunlit street, felt both foolish and conspicuous, as though he had succumbed to the temptation of some appalling vice. The cane looked so new. At school it had been the worst possible form to have an unblemished leather trunk with bright buckles: the thing had been to kick it, or to drop it several times from luggage van on to station platform. Now, he felt like a soldier who had not yet been to France, because of the cane: people looked at him and he wanted to shout at them, 'I have been before, I have been and now I am going back. I *know*.'

There was nothing that he could think of to do. Outside Victoria, crowds of women and soldiers and children gripped hard by the hand. An old woman in a black veil fed the pigeons. The heat was unbearable, striking up from the pavement. He had not eaten and did not want to eat. There were three hours before his train.

And so he went into the shadow of the station, where it was a little cooler, and found a bench and sat, his cases and the cane walking-stick beside him, sat for three hours. At first he bought a paper, and did not read it, bought an orange from a barrow, and did not eat it. Only watched the gleaming trains come in and go out under the vaulted roof and saw, beyond it, the curve of blue sky. He felt nothing, no particular fear or despair.

The world came and went, then, for three hours, inside Victoria station. Men departed for the front and returned from it and he saw those who came with them to say goodbye, and those who walked in agitation up and down the platforms, waiting, saw partings and greetings, saw the waving and the tears. He thought of his own farewell to his mother, remembered her still figure in the cream-coloured dress. Once or twice he made as if to move, to get up and stretch his legs, go for a drink in the bar, walk outside and take a look at the sky and the pigeons and the taxi-cabs, but in the end he did not, he simply sat, watching.

There was a good deal about which he might have thought, and he wondered why he did not do so. There were memories: last night's quiet beach, the faces of his family, Henry Partington. Or there might so easily have been anger, at the things he had heard and read in England about the conduct of the war: he could have despised the Major, who was going blind and fed his dog and felt out of things, who would have thought something of Hilliard if he had gone for the cavalry. Or could have pitied him.

He wondered, too, why he did not think ahead, as he had done yesterday, about his own platoon, and what had been going on and what would go on during the coming autumn. He thought nothing. A few yards off a man in a frock coat fidgeted with a carnation in his button-hole and, when he was satisfied with the set of it, took out a handkerchief and because of grief or heat wiped his eyes carefully, before he walked away.

It was like being under water or some mild anaesthetic, everything around Hilliard and within him was remote, people parted and moved and reformed in bright, regular patterns like fragments in a kaleidoscope.

After more than an hour he felt a strange contentment begin to seep through him. He was quite relaxed. He had left Hawton, where he had been so unhappy, and his future movements would be decided for him by other people in some other place. He had only to follow. There would be no more anxieties about what he should or should not let himself say to them at home, or about whose names he might read in the lists in the newspapers, about how he could bear to sit in the sour-smelling room with the Major, tensed with dread of the night to come, of his dreams and the open window letting in the scent of roses.

'What would you like for lunch, John?'

'Is there anything I can get you from the library?'

'Do you want to be woken for church in the morning, or shall I leave you?'

'Is your leg healed enough for you to try and swim?'

'Your father says you'll be back by Christmas, it will certainly be all over. Is he right? Do you agree with him?'

'Shall I marry Henry Partington? Do you approve, John?'

'What would you like for dinner, John?'

No more of that. He would only get their letters, as faint reminders of some other world. Instead, he would be making entirely possible decisions, about maps and marches and the conditions of rifles and feet, he would be taking simple orders about life and death.

He felt a moment of singing happiness.

Most of the men stayed on deck for a long time, watching the lights and rooftops of the town disappearing behind them. The boat was very full and it was easy, he now realized, to pick out the ones who had been here before, so that he ceased to worry about the silver-topped cane. Instead, he lay down across two wooden-slatted chairs, using his valise as a pillow, and, after a while, slept. He did not dream. Around him men talked and played cards, drank and read and sang, or were alert, silent.

When he awoke, he saw the sea immediately in front of his face through glass, and the sky, white as a gull's belly, and, for a moment, it seemed that he was asleep on the beach at Hawton, that nothing had passed between his last walk there in the moonlight and this dawn. But when he sat up he saw the houses of Cherbourg. His back was aching. He was very hungry.

'Mr Hilliard ...'

'Coulter! Good evening.' For a second, he had not remembered the man's name, but he was delighted to see a familiar face, to feel that he was almost home.

'How are you, sir?'

'Better. Very well, thanks. I was expecting Bates. Where is he?'

Coulter frowned, shaking his head, but for a moment, Hilliard did not take in his meaning.

'Excuse me for just a moment, sir, there are some men I've to look out for. We've had reinforcements this week – not before time. If you wouldn't mind holding on, sir.'

They were standing in the early evening sunlight, on the grass beside the train. No station, no buildings, only a stopping place, this. Other men peered down at them through the smeared windows, waiting to travel on. Hilliard had only a rough idea of where he was. The train had taken over seven hours but that meant nothing, they had stopped and crawled, stopped and crawled. Only once he thought he recognized a town they went through and then a village, a part of the countryside, white châteaux with green shutters glimpsed through some trees.

The message for him at Cherbourg had been that his battalion was at a rest-camp, twenty miles behind the front line. So they must have come down after Pourville Wood. More than that he could not know. Except that he had expected his own batman, Bates, to meet him and take him on, and here was Coulter, whom he scarcely knew – a small man with a crumpled, old-young face. Hilliard tried to remember something about him.

It was very quiet. Ahead of him, the road ran down, dusty-white, between sloping fields. The trees were as parched as they had been at home, but much yellower, here it was already autumn. The sun glinted on the weather-vane of a church, just visible behind a copse in the far distance, and it was bright as a shell in the night sky. But silent.

'If you're ready now, sir?'

Coulter picked up his bags. Behind them, a group of men, all of them new to France. Hilliard saw that they looked tired, though it was only because of the heat and the tedious journey, but they were excited, too, willing and keen. Incredibly young. Coulter had organized them, they began to walk. The train stood where it was.

He wanted to say, Do I look older than that? Do I look as old as I feel?

'Glad to see you looking fit, sir.'

'Thanks.'

'All right walking now, are you?'

'Oh, yes, yes. Fine.'

'It's not so far away. Mile and a half.'

'How long have we been down here?'

'Best part of a week, sir. It's a nice place, I must say. Very pleasant.'

They passed down the hill between sun-soaked trees, and the gnats and midges hovered in thick, dark clusters. The road narrowed, became a lane. There were dried cart rucks along the edges. A rabbit shot across a few yards ahead of them, and stopped in the middle of the road, ears quivering, waited. It's like going back to school, Hilliard thought, it's so bloody peaceful, it's like going back to school, with a prefect to lead you up the road from the station because you're new, you don't know the way, you haven't been here before. Except that he had.

The rabbit stayed until they came within a few feet of it before making in panic for the brambles.

'Where's the war, Coulter?'

The man smiled. Behind, the new recruits to the Battalion. They were not talking.

'How many for B Company?'

'Eight, sir. We had forty, last week, and ten just before we came down.'

'*What?*'

'Not enough. We're still well under strength.'

'What's been happening, for God's sake?'

'Don't you know, sir?'

They rounded a bend. Somewhere he could hear water.

'Coulter?'

'You'll find out about it all, the C.O.'ll tell you, soon enough. He's been waiting for someone new to tell.'

'It was hopeless trying to make any sense out of the newspaper reports.'

'I'll bet, sir!'

'They garble everything, it's all lies, you can't work out who's doing what, who's where – who won.'

Coulter looked at him sideways. *Won,* sir?'

'Well – yes, I saw the lists.'

'Yes, sir.'

'Bates?'

'Oh yes, sir. Most of your platoon. Most of the Company, really, sir. You won't find many faces you know, sir.'

Bates had been his batman from the beginning. A bad-tempered man, strong as an ox, entirely reliable. Hilliard had trusted Bates, and liked him, too, because the war had not changed him, he was morose as he had always been, he was an Old Army man, apparently indestructible.

'There's a new Adjutant, sir. Captain Franklin – B Company.'

'Yes.'

He had read Captain Ward's name in one of the first Casualty Lists after he had returned to England. Ward and

Houghton, Fane, Bryant, Anderson and Sergeant-Major Pearcy. And Mason-Godwin, who had shared a hut with him that spring in Training Camp, had gone into the artillery.

'They gave him the M.C.! Captain Ward, that is, sir. Came through just after you left. Did you know that? A day or two before he was killed. He went up with a mine, sir. See that red roof just to your left, behind the dip? That's the place. Manor house, it was, and a farm alongside. Yes, very pleasant it is, sir.'

The sky was rose-red, and darkening at the edges as the sun dropped down.

'Been hot, sir, I can tell you that.'

'And at home.'

'Yes, so Mrs Phipps writes.'

Then he remembered about Coulter: that he had no family at all, had been brought up in an orphanage, from which he had run away at the age of eleven, to join the circus. His only letters came from a friend and his wife who travelled England with a team of performing monkeys. Coulter was a happy man, self-sufficient, small and hard as a nut.

'I daresay you enjoyed your time at home, sir.'

'Yes,' Hilliard said. 'Yes, thank you.'

They turned up the long drive through orchards of pear and apple. The fruit was thick, and brown and much of it lay in the long grass, rotting.

The main building was three-storeyed and built of red brick, with two large wings at right angles, and a number of barns, stables and outhouses and, further down the road, some cottages. Beyond and between them, in the fields and orchards, green tents. Smoke was rising from the chimneys in pale, thin plumes. But it was the lull at the end of the day, there was for the time being no other sign of life.

Hilliard felt suddenly tired. But excited, too, he wanted to see everyone, hear everything, even the worst, he felt at home even though he had never been to this place before. He thought, it's like going back to school.

'Most of your platoon. Most of the Company, really, sir. You won't find many faces you know.'

'The C.O. asked to see you, sir, when you've settled in. And there's a new second lieutenant attached to your platoon. Came three days ago. Mr Barton, his name. He's sharing with you, sir, we're a bit short of space here even if we are under strength. And I'll be serving for both of you, sir, for the time being, anyway.'

Hilliard felt irrationally angry. He wanted a corner to himself, even though he knew that was the one thing you never got, in France. He wanted his own room like the one overlooking the rose garden at Hawton, not an attic or an outhouse shared with another subaltern. A stranger.

They had come into the front yard of the main building. A mongrel-dog, rough-coated and dirty, was lying across the cobbles, chewing a bone, happy to stay in familiar territory and be petted by the army. Hilliard thought how ludicrous it was to be here, in the last of the evening light, standing before these red-tiled, serviceable country buildings, how ludicrous that it should be so quiet, that there should be grass and apple trees and the smell of cooking, a dog and blackbirds. That there should seem, apart from the young recruits behind him and the short, uniformed figure of Coulter, to be nobody here at all, no Battalion, no front line trenches twenty miles away, no guns, no armies in the country. No war.

He followed Coulter, feeling the silver knob of his stick warm and hard in the ball of his hand. The cane was already scuffed and dirty.

Coulter was right about the overcrowding. B and D Companies were together at the farm which was also serving as Battalion Headquarters, but the rest were in the village of Percelle, half a mile down the lane. It had been badly shelled that spring, Coulter said, there was scarcely an unshattered roof over anybody's head. But because of the good weather and because at last they were away from the front line, here, where it was so quiet, nobody complained.

When Hilliard stood upright in the room he was to share with the new second lieutenant, he cracked his head on a rafter. This was part of the loft, reached by a wooden ladder that came up through the floor. For years, apples and pears had been stored here and although there was no fruit now, the juice had soaked and stained the boards, so that every so often, as one trod them, there came up an old, faint smell of cider.

Coulter had left him after having brought up water in an enamel bowl. Above his head the roof light was propped open, showing a square of damson-dark sky. As he unstrapped his case to find soap and razor, he heard, for the first time since his return, the boom of guns. But they seemed very far away, they had sounded more clearly than that sometimes at Hawton, when the wind was blowing off the sea.

The bugle had gone for the men to eat, he had heard shouts and footsteps on the farmyard cobbles below, and once, the grind of a motor, coming up the long drive.

The narrow apple loft might have been a corner of a dormitory. Below, the sounds of the other boys, settling in. *It's like bloody well going back to school.*

And then he looked across at the other man's belongings, resenting their presence. He was not anxious to acquaint himself with this stranger.

BARTON D.J.C.B. COY. 2ND BATTALION,
THE ROYAL – RGT B.E.F. FRANCE

The lettering was upright and plain and clear, done in black ink. The leather of the valise still shone, the buckles were not yet tarnished. There was a tortoise-shell backed hairbrush and comb, and a slab of Chocolate Menier. A copy of *The Turn of the Screw* and of the complete works of Sir Thomas Browne, and one of the Psalms, bound in navy morocco. Hilliard reached out a hand towards it, hesitated, drew his hand back.

On top of the trunk which served as a table beside the camp-bed, a double-folding photograph wallet. The back was to him, he could not see without touching it what faces were inside. He did not touch. Instead, he turned away, made preparations to shave. The sound of the motor vehicle going away again. Footsteps. But no one came up the wooden ladder.

Putting his hand into the bowl of water, he found that it was warm, and thought how he would remember once they were back at the front, the luxury of shaving in warm water from a clean bowl. At home, he had not been able to get over it at first, the simple availability of water, for washing, shaving, bathing, drinking – for wasting. He had turned on the taps in the bathroom and splashed drinking water again and again over his face, let it slide coolly down his wrists, wondering at it. For so long, there had been only the tins of green water, stinking of chlorine, to drink, and the grey scum in which someone else had washed before him and the foul water at the bottom of shell holes, before the sun of June and July had come to dry them out. He remembered the men brought in wounded and set down in the bottom of the trench, or being taken up on stretchers, who were crying out not only from pain and fear, but for water. At Neuville, he had sent five emergency messages up the communication trench demanding more water, more water. It had not come. The sixth time, they had sent a runner who was hit, and the water can had burst open and spilled on to the soil beside him.

Hilliard lifted the dripping wet shaving brush up to his face.

He could not get used to what the C.O. looked like. He sat on the opposite side of the table, with the wide windows, overlooking the orchard, behind him. It was not dark yet but the lamp was already lit. Perhaps it was that, he thought, perhaps Garrett looked better in the undistorting daylight. But it was not that, not just an expression. Everything about him had changed.

'Hilliard!' He had almost cried out his name, and come quickly across the room to greet him, and it was as though he had been sitting here, for hours or days, awaiting his return. Here was one familiar face, someone who had survived.

'How are you? I hope they haven't cut your time short? I hope they've seen to it that you're properly fit?'

Yes, he said, yes they had, yes he was fit, no, there was nothing wrong at all, the leg was more than healed. And all the time, he stared at the Colonel.

'I'm surprised they didn't send me back sooner – a week ago. It seems you could have done with me.'

Garrett turned and gave him a curious look. But he only said, 'No. You needed the rest'

He went over to a cupboard, took out glasses and a bottle of whisky. Hilliard saw other bottles, gleaming darkly behind it. The C.O. had developed a strange half-limp, but it seemed not to be the result of any physical injury, rather of agitation. He moved a hand up to his head, smoothing back the hair nervously again and again, while the other poured drink into the glasses.

'Soda?'

'If you have it?'

'I suppose we do. Yes.'

'Water will do.'

'No, no. There's soda. I saw it. I'm positive there was some soda. It's Keefe, he moves things, he's a damned nuisance. Tidies everything. He's obsessed with tidiness.'

Hilliard had never heard him complain like that, like a peevish old man.

'You don't know Keefe.'

'No.'

'There won't be many you do know.'

Garrett was sorting helplessly among the bottles and glasses in the cupboard.

'This is perfectly all right, sir. Don't trouble about the soda.'

'No? Well, I don't seem to be able to find it. Perhaps there wasn't any.'

'This is fine.' Though he had forgotten how strong neat whisky could be against the back of his throat.

'Keefe moves everything, blast it.'

He came back, fidgeted with some papers, moved the lamp, sat down in the end. Hilliard thought, I have been away five weeks and he is twenty years older, he is ... He could not take it in.

From the beginning of his time here he had liked Colonel Garrett, had got on well with him, though without holding him in the same sort of esteem he had held Ward, the dead Captain of B Company. But the C.O. had befriended him, had seen that he was as comfortable as any man could be, that spring on the Somme. He made a point of keeping in touch, of sending for and talking to his subalterns as well as the senior officers, he came down into the trenches frequently.

Garrett had trained as a lawyer before taking his army commission and he still seemed much more like a solicitor than a soldier, though he had been in the army for so long. Hilliard wondered why he *was* in the army. He knew that Garrett had a wife and four daughters somewhere, in Worthing or Horsham or Lewes. He was not an imaginative man. But careful, a good planner, cool headed. Perhaps all that simply meant, brave.

Within the space of five weeks, and those after two years of consistent service in the Old Front Line, his air of calm and the slight ponderousness had vanished. His face was altered, was thinner, the eyes puffed but the cheeks drawn in, his fingers moved all the time about the rim of his glass, or smoothed down the patch of thinning hair. Mons, Le Cateau and Ypres, and then the first battle of the spring offensive had not shaken him. So what had the past month been like? Hilliard was appalled, he had not dreamed that this could happen and so quickly to a man like Garrett. To a man who was yet not ill or wounded, who had survived for so long by careful management, perhaps, and luck. Well, and he still survived, he was here. An old man in the yellow-grey lamplight.

It was possible to see what this room of the farmhouse had been like as a parlour: there was a wide stone fireplace and an uneven floor, you could imagine old soft sofas and coarse mats, stone jugs full of marigolds and cornflowers. The windows, long and loose in their frames, shaken by past shelling, were open now. The smells of the autumn evening came in, of grass and trees and rotting fruit, and the army smells, tobacco and bullet smoke, horses and cooking.

The guns were booming like summer thunder, away in the distance.

'You lost Bates, of course.'

'Yes.'

'I think Coulter's a good man, isn't he? You'll be all right with Coulter.'

'Yes.'

For a moment, he wondered whether nothing else might be said, whether Garrett would not want, after all, to go over what had happened, preferring to leave the summer behind him. There were too many names to bring up, too many individual deaths.

Silence. The C.O. jerked his head and looked behind him suddenly, as though he had heard something unusual, and then turned back again. Hilliard could not get over his face, the change in his face. He waited for the usual questions about home.

'We lost three quarters of the Battalion in a day and a half. Getting on for two dozen officers. Major Gadney, young Parkinson, Ward – all the best. Half of them went because we didn't receive an order telling us the second push was cancelled. They just went on. You were well out of it. I'm glad you were out of it.'

Hilliard did not speak.

'I've seen nothing like it. Nothing. Not that we were the

only ones. They went mad, we might have been a pack of
schoolboys in a scrum. Did you hear about the Jocks? Most
of them went straight on to the wire. They were on our
right, we watched it. The sun was shining, you could see
for miles, even through the smoke, we just watched them
go. We lost Pearcy and thirty-eight men all in one go. I'd
just gone down there, I saw them. God alone knows what
was supposed to be going on. I didn't. I haven't found out
yet. None of us knows. I suppose it's all on paper somewhere. Nothing came through to us at all, everything
went to blazes, telephones, runners. Half the artillery
blew themselves up with their own Lewis guns backfir-
ing because somebody hadn't attended to them properly.
Most of Parkinson's lot went up with a mine. There was a
barrage they didn't tell us about and we couldn't get word
through to them to stop, we were running into our own
covering fire. And then they started to shoot machine guns
from the left flank, they'd lost their bearings, they thought
we were Boche. Not surprising. After an hour or so you
couldn't see a thing. It was a day and a half, two days, of
absolute bloody chaos. Bloody pointless mess.'

Hilliard realized that this was what had upset his
careful, lawyer's mind more than anything else, this lack
of order and reason. The mess.

'And then we had another full week without any relief,
and most of our support line gone.'

All the time he spoke he turned the whisky glass round
and round in his hand, so that the lamplight caught it.
Hilliard could not piece the story together, could not

picture what might have happened in the battle, any more than Garrett could remember. He did not even know exactly when it had been. It did not matter. He had only to listen.

'It was about eighty degrees during the day. I've never known it so hot.'

He remembered the heat, in the ward of the military hospital. They had pulled down the green blinds but it had felt no cooler. The Field-Gunner had tossed about, crying all day as he cried all night.

'You were well out of it.'

'Yes.'

'Clifford went berserk. Do you remember Clifford? Swarthy looking chap, bit of a gypsy. Went completely berserk, they couldn't hold him down, couldn't shut him up, couldn't do anything with him at all.'

'Was he hurt?'

'No.'

'What happened in the end, then?'

'Oh, he shot himself.'

Garrett's voice trailed off. Hilliard did not remember the man, Clifford, but that did not matter, either. He wondered how long it was since Garrett had talked so freely. Talked at all. He could not say anything either at Brigade Headquarters, or to the newcomers. He had been waiting for Hilliard.

Then, he seemed to come to abruptly, and his eyes refocused. He said, 'Well, what about you? You seem all right.'

'I am, thank you, sir.'

'Home?'

'Fine, thanks.'

'I'm due for a turn of leave. Doesn't look as if I'll get it, not yet, anyway.'

No, and better not, Hilliard wanted to say, you had far better stay here, in this farmhouse among the apple trees. Don't go back to London, to England, don't go and listen to what they say and read their papers, don't try and talk to them as you are talking to me, for there is nobody, no one knows. Don't go.

But that was not right. For Garrett was not like him. He would enjoy all the time he spent with his wife and family, would play golf and stroke the cat and go for a week to Cowes or Ventnor, and up to London to see a show, would drink malt whisky and China tea and eat in good restaurants, stay in the most comfortable hotels, would close his eyes and ears to what he did not want to see and hear, and his mind to what he wanted to forget. If he could. So much had changed, he was changed, he would not belong in England now. None of them belonged there. And Garrett had lost his faith.

Hilliard felt a wave of misery, that there was no one left and, of those who were, Garrett could no longer be relied upon. Garrett had been like a rivet, hard and secure, down the back of the Battalion.

He finished his whisky. The guns thundered. It had gone quite dark.

'Have you met Mr Barton yet?'

As soon as he put his foot on the bottom rung of the loft ladder, he could see the other man's shadow above him. Then he heard a board creak, as Barton walked across the room. Hilliard waited. He had never felt it before, this irrational disinclination to come face to face with someone. He was not shy though he did not make close friends. He had found his feet easily enough in the army, from the beginning. There were always new arrivals, changes, people to get used to, just as there had been at school. Some he liked, some he was indifferent to, a few he detested. As was normal. He knew nothing at all about the new subaltern except that Garrett had said. 'Pleasant young chap. Lively.' BARTON D.J.C. He had been here three days.

There was no further sound from above. He would have to go up, it was almost time for dinner. The large measure of whisky had made him slightly giddy.

Oh, for heaven's sake ...

But he did not want to meet Barton. He wasn't going to like him.

He went very quickly up the ladder.

Barton had his back to him, was reading a letter.

'Good evening.'

At once the other man turned, said, 'Hilliard?' with pleasure. Hilliard stood upright in the loft and cracked his head again on the beam.

Barton grinned. '*I've* been doing that for three days! You think you won't forget it another time but you generally do.'

He came across and shook hands. There was a lamp on

the small table which lit up only the immediate area encircling it, and cast long fingers of shadow on to the wooden roof. The corners of the loft were in darkness. Hilliard could not see him distinctly, the side of his head blocked out the light.

'I saw your things. I knew you'd arrived.' He hesitated. 'To tell you the truth, I was frightened to death of you!'

At once, Hilliard felt a wave of relief, coupled with an instinctive suspicion. It was all very well to feel something, to think it, but not to say so openly. 'I was frightened to death of you.' He himself would never have said, 'I didn't want to meet you, I thought I was going to dislike you.' He realized now, that he had been quite wrong.

Barton was younger than himself, though Hilliard was uncertain by how much, and he was more than a head taller. He had a particularly deep voice, with a faint hint of amusement in it, not at Hilliard but at himself.

He said, 'I was just going down.'

'Yes, we better had. I've been talking to the C.O.'

'He told me rather a lot about you as soon as I got here. He was wanting to have you back.'

Hilliard brushed the sleeve of his tunic.

'He thinks a lot of you, doesn't he?'

'I really don't know.'

At once he was ashamed of himself for being so curt. But there was an openness about Barton which for some reason made him uneasy.

'You carry on,' he said, 'I'll join you.'

Barton hesitated. Then moved towards the ladder.

In the officers' dining room, which had been the old dining room of the farmhouse and still retained the long refectory table, the light was better, he could see Barton clearly. He did not seem a man who would ever attract dislike. He was not quite twenty, and he looked older because he was mature, in complete possession of himself. It was not the premature ageing that often came to those who had been a short time at the front. He had some kind of central poise and calmness. But all around that, on the surface, nothing was calm or still, he talked easily and quickly, smiled, laughed at himself and, on all sides, attracted a response. Attracted, simply, liking. He did not seem a stranger, among all those here who were strangers. Looking around him, Hilliard realized for the first time exactly how many had gone.

He found himself watching Barton, listening, he felt drawn into the circle of his attention. He was talking about some relative, an aunt, who dashed about the Warwickshire countryside on a horse, riding astride not side-saddle, wearing breeches not skirts, to the horror of all who met with her. She was called Eustacia.

'Only we none of us could ever say it properly, we all called her You-Stay-Shy. We still do.'

We?

Barton was cutting a wedge of cheese. He looked up for a moment, catching Hilliard's eye. His own were a curious green-blue, under a low forehead and thick, black hair. His voice was still full of amusement.

'The best thing is, she's had nine children to date and I

shouldn't have thought there's anything at all to stop her having another nine, in between the hunting seasons.'

What is it, Hilliard thought, why are we all listening and laughing and waiting for more? Is it that he is simply very young and new to this place, has no idea at all of the future, of what it is really like, and so there is still time left, a short time, for him to entertain us. He has seen nothing, he can talk in this way and assume that we have nothing else to occupy our thoughts. We might simply be out to dinner at some hotel in England, a party of officers on leave. The wine, reasonably good wine, was going round the table freely. He felt light-headed and warm, companionable, even among so many strangers, in the lamplight. He saw Colonel Garrett watching Barton too, and although the terrible change was still so noticeable on his face, he was more relaxed, smiling occasionally, in his old, tight way, he was clearly anxious for Barton to continue.

The others, the few who were left that he knew, had greeted Hilliard warmly enough, had said a word or two about what he had missed, and then changed the subject, hurried to eat and drink and introduce him to the strangers. To the new Adjutant, Franklin. A particularly tall man. Now, Hilliard saw that it was only Franklin whose attention was not wholly taken up with Barton's story. He leaned back in his chair, one hand resting on the table in front of him, a blank, faintly detached expression on his face. He did not look at Barton, did not smile, was drinking little. Hilliard wondered where he had come from.

'I'm going to write out a neat little notice, PLEASE LOWER

YOUR HEAD. I shall get Coulter to nail it up, else Hilliard and I will have our brains bashed in before we get near any guns.'

He was still smiling. Hilliard stiffened, waited for someone to express, by a look or gesture, disapproval of the remark. For did they want to be reminded of the front line, of skulls cracked and brains spilled, here, tonight and by this new young subaltern, who had seen nothing, knew nothing?

He felt himself suddenly ready to defend Barton, as he might defend a younger boy at school who had blurted out something because he did not yet know the form. He thought, we need him, he has something none of us have, we need him to stay here, just as he is, to sit here night after night, telling us his stories, or nodding in that way he nods when someone else talks, sympathetic, happy to yield the floor – *liking us*. For there is little enough left of what he has. And what is that? What is that?

He caught Barton's eye and Barton smiled. The C.O. was talking. Hilliard looked away, filled with unease.

The glasses and cutlery were cleared, Garrett brought papers, a map, he had things to tell them. Barton listened with great concentration, his body completely still, head turned towards the Colonel. Hilliard looked at him once and then did not do so again. He thought, *what is it?*

It was gone ten o'clock when they broke up from the conference around the dining table, and Hilliard wanted to get outside, after the wine he had drunk and the stuffiness

from oil lamps and tobacco smoke. In one of the two large
sitting rooms of the house, which served as an officers'
mess, someone had put on a gramophone record of *The
Mikado.* Upstairs, in his valise, there was 'The Favourite
Selection from Gilbert and Sullivan,' bound in green cloth
with gold lettering on the cover, bought as a present for
Reevely, who had sung so badly and who was dead. Hilliard
wondered what he was going to do with the music now.

He stood for a moment in the doorway of the farmhouse. From the stables, the sound of buckets clanking,
as the horses were fed and watered for the night: from a
barn, some of the men, singing; someone shouted to the
dog. He stepped out on to the cobbles and breathed in the
smoky smell of night. Someone came up behind him in
the doorway.

'Do you play cards, Hilliard?'

Captain Franklin. His face was curiously expressionless. He had hair and moustache of a pale brown, like
gingerbread.

'I don't really, sir.'

'Not even whist?'

'I'm no good at it.'

'No good at bridge then, I suppose?'

'I'm afraid not.'

'Pity. We need someone to make up a four. Barton's no
use either.'

'Sorry.'

'All right.'

Hilliard felt that it was not all right.

'Are you going out?'

'I think I need to stretch my legs, yes.'

'You might walk over to the stables for me, see if Preston's there and ask him to keep an eye on my horse's leg. He'll know.' He paused for a moment, and then added in the same tone, 'If you're going that way.'

'Of course.'

Hilliard was irritated, he felt that the Adjutant had been putting him to some sort of test, because the message sounded unnecessary, and in any case he could perfectly well have sent his batman across with it. It had been mid-way between an order and a request for Hilliard to do him a favour. But then, there was no reason why he should not, in fact, be 'going that way'.

The stables were warm and the smell of hay and manure was nostalgic to him, even though his acquaintance with it only went back as far as that spring, in Wiltshire. They were good stables here, roomy and solid. The Company's horses did not seem to be so overcrowded as the men.

He opened the half-door and stepped inside. A Tilley lamp stood high up on the window ledge.

'Mr Hilliard!'

'Hello, Preston, how are you?'

The usual questions, the usual replies. But he was glad that here was someone he knew still left.

Preston had been a stable boy at Newmarket, and Hilliard suspected that he was under age when he joined up the previous year. But he looked after the Company's horses as though they were all being carefully primed for the next race. Hilliard had once asked him if he did not feel these animals to be greatly inferior to the thoroughbreds he was used to. Preston had looked shocked. They were horses, so it was all one, they were what he cared about.

'Captain Franklin wanted me to give you a message?'

'Yes, sir?'

'Apparently there's something wrong with his horse's leg?'

Preston did not reply, but turned away and picked up a bucket. The animals moved about, humped against their stalls, tossing their heads up now and again quietly.

'Anyway, he wanted you to keep an eye on it.'

Preston was slight, with a thin face and quick movements. He had little personality and little to say for himself, unless it were on the subject of horses, but there was an air of cleverness about him. He preferred to be in the infantry, though he could have gone into transport, where he would have had more to do with horses and less with everything else. Hilliard sensed that he either resented Franklin's message or was scornful of it, but his face gave nothing away, nothing was said at all.

'We're for the front again next week, aren't we, sir?'

'Are we?'

'So they say.'

'You seem to know all about it.'

Preston slapped the thick flank of a horse. It champed on at the hay basket, unperturbed.

'Well, I shan't mind, I like being where there's something going on, I suppose. I get fed up here, waiting around.'

'Were you at Neuville?'

'Oh yes, sir.' He sounded casual. 'You missed all that, didn't you? Never a dull moment!'

Hilliard could not take it in. Perhaps Preston had been in one of the quieter bits? But no, none of them had because there had been no quiet bits that summer. Was he unaffected, then? Did he think nothing of what he had seen? Was he blunted, or simply resilient? It could be that he was unimaginative. But you had not needed imagination.

'You were in Parkinson's platoon, weren't you?'

Preston glanced over his shoulder as he reached for the Tilley lamp. It swung, flickering momentarily over the eyes and nostrils of the horses. That's right, sir. There were just two of us left, me and Andrews.' He lifted the lamp up and moved it along the line of animals, taking a last look at each of them in turn. As he did so, his expression altered.

'Most of these have come to us new,' he said, 'we lost all the others. They've no right to make horses suffer in a war, not the way those did. They don't choose to come out here, do they? All I do is try not to think about it, so much. It bothers me, thinking about it, sir.'

His voice was the same, the flat, Cambridgeshire accent, and his face looked ferret-like, seen in profile above the lamp. He means it, Hilliard thought, he just means what he says. That he tries not to think about the dead horses.

It did not seem wrong, then, that this should be so. He had forgotten how much he himself had come to like the horses.

'Had you no ambition to go for the cavalry?'

He had not, for he saw no point to it, in this war, but none of that would have made any sense to the Major.

'Don't forget about Captain Franklin's horse then.'

'There's nothing wrong with Captain Franklin's horse that decent riding won't put right again.'

'Preston!'

'Sorry, sir. Yes, I'll go and take a look at it now, sir.'

'All right.'

As Hilliard stepped out of the stables, he heard the splashing sound of a horse beginning to urinate against the stone floor.

Ahead of him, the shadow of a man, standing at the top of the drive.

'Hilliard?'

Barton.

'I thought I'd walk with you for a bit if that's all right.' His voice was friendly.

Hilliard had thought that what he wanted was to be alone, to go down between the fruit trees and into the dark lane and get his bearings. But now, with Barton standing in front of him, he realized that he did not, that he had had more than enough of walking by himself, of his own thoughts and memories and despair, had had too much solitariness, at Hawton.

He said, 'Yes, do.'

Barton fell into step with him on the rough farmyard path. Away to the west, a succession of green Verey flares lit up the sky, followed by the guns. Then it went black again, as they came down into the lane facing a belt of trees. Again, Hilliard heard the sound of water.

'If we go up here and turn off to the left we come into another orchard. It leads across to the church eventually. There's a bit of a stream.'

Hilliard nodded and they went that way. The air smelled damp, there might be some mist at dawn.

He thought I should remember this, I should remember everything about it, for it will not last. At once, the atmosphere around him seemed too insubstantial to be remembered, it was nothing, was only a walk between trees and through long grass at night, there were the usual sounds and smells, the hidden movements of small creatures in the undergrowth. There was nothing in particular to remember. And everything.

'*We're for the front again next week, sir.*'

The men always heard rumours and the rumours spread and turned out to be the truth.

Their footsteps swished through the grass. They came nearer to the sound of water.

'I'm glad you've come,' Barton said easily.

They went as far as the edge of the stream and then sat down, leaning against some willows. Barton lit a cigarette and the sparks flickered upwards through the leaves of the tree. His eyes and the lower half of his face were in darkness, but the line of his nose, with its high, narrow bridge, gleamed bone-white. The tree trunks were like pewter.

Looking at him, Hilliard thought that Barton was handsome, and that he would have liked to introduce him to

Beth. That thought had never occurred to him with any man before, probably because he had taken so few friends home. But he dismissed the idea almost at once, for Beth was too old, was twenty-four, was plain and about to marry the lawyer Henry Partington. Thinking of the new person she had become, he knew that she would not understand anything about Barton. He was not sure if he did so himself. But he wanted to understand. Beth might not.

'I didn't expect it to be like this,' Barton was saying. His knees were up to his chin, head forward as he looked at the water. 'I'd heard all the things you do hear about the war. I hadn't expected it to be such a pleasant life.'

'We are in rest camp, you know.'

You wait, he should be saying, you wait. But where was the point of that? Barton would find out, soon enough.

'All the same, it's a bit like being back at O.T.C. Rather boring. I thought at least we'd be under shell fire or sharing a room with some rats.'

'Is that what you were looking forward to?'

'Oh God, no!'

'Then why say it? And this won't last for ever.'

'No. I didn't want to come out here at all, I was in a blue funk. I'd have done more or less anything … but I'm fit and of age, I couldn't slip through the net. So I suppose I'd better make the most of it.'

'Do you always tell people everything you're feeling?'

Barton looked round at him in surprise. 'Generally. If I want to. If they want to hear.' He paused and then laughed. 'Good Lord, we're not at school now, are we?'

Hilliard did not reply.

'Besides, it's the way we were brought up. To say things, tell people what you feel. I don't mean to force it on anyone. But not to bottle things up.'

'I see.'

'It's my father mainly. He's pretty busy so we might easily go through life seeing hardly anything of him. He makes a point of seeing each of us alone, for a while, every week, find out what we're doing, asking if we've anything to tell him, you know? It's a bit like having an appointment in his surgery really!'

'He's a doctor?'

'Yes.'

'When you say "we …"'

'There are six of us. Three brothers older than me, two sisters, younger. We all came tumbling one after another though, so we seem much of an age. It's good that way, especially now. We've always been close, of course, but when you're small children you just take that for granted, don't you?'

Do you? Hilliard tried to decide. Yes, he had been close to Beth. But that had changed, now they were older, separated.

He said, 'I have one sister.'

'Younger?'

'No, she's twenty-four. '

'Is she married?'

'She – not yet.'

'Tell her to get a move on, then you can have all your nephews and nieces – you'll enjoy that.'

'Shall I?'

'Oh, of course. I do. I get on with my sisters best, I think. Both of them are married now.'

Barton slid down the tree trunk into the grass, resting on his arm. 'No, I withdraw that, there's really no difference between any of us, we all live out of one another's pockets. And the brothers-in-law now. They've just been absorbed into the family! I shan't like it being out here and not seeing any of them. We're all so split up now.'

'Haven't your brothers joined up?'

'One's got exemption because he has tuberculosis. Dick's in the R.A.M.C. but he's gone out to Egypt. My youngest brother's in prison.' He talked about them as though he had never in his life found any reason to keep things back. Hilliard was slightly embarrassed.

'He's a conchy. I nearly was, but then I realized it was nothing to do with conscience, it was just because I was frightened and wanted to get out of coming to France. Edward's different, he really means it. He put up a terrific fight, and he's having a rotten time, it isn't much fun for him. I'm better off than he is, at the moment.'

What he felt most of all was envy of Barton. He tried to picture what it would be like to have a family, to whom you were so close, about whom you could talk so lovingly, people you missed every day, and admitted to missing. What would it feel like? What kind of people were they, all these Bartons? What did they say and do together?

'I suppose you didn't much want to come back either, did you? Especially since you already know what it's like?'

'I don't … ' But there seemed no way he could begin to explain, not without telling everything about himself. He had never done that.

Barton had moved forward and was leaning his arm down into the stream. 'This is pretty well dried up,' he said thoughtfully. 'I wonder how long since it rained?'

Something seemed to click inside Hilliard. It was all right. Barton was all right. He could talk, after all, could tell him anything.

'I didn't mind coming back,' he said. 'It was so bloody awful at home. I couldn't stick it. Not that I forgot what it had been like out here – I had nightmares about it. Nobody ever forgets. But I couldn't bear to stay on at home, to stay in England at all, it's … I can't explain. I wish I could tell you.'

'Tell me,' Barton said simply. He still lay on his stomach, hand dabbling gently in the water. His legs were very long, reaching back through the grass towards Hilliard.

He had been waiting for someone, just as Garrett had waited for him. Waiting for Barton. Though he had not known it. Long ago, he would have talked to Beth. Not now. There had never been anyone else close enough.

'Go on. Tell me.'

Hilliard did so. It was not difficult after all.

When he had finished, Barton lay without moving, his head resting on the grass now, both arms outstretched. Hilliard wondered if he had fallen asleep. His own voice seemed to have gone on for so long, he had never talked so much. But if he expected some comment, none came. For a long time, they were both silent. A breeze came from somewhere behind them, rustling the willow leaves like silk. A few of them drifted down on to Hilliard's shoulders and into the water.

He did not want to have to move from here. All the anxiety he had felt for so many weeks, longer than he could really remember, had left him, but the effects of the wine he had drunk earlier were quite gone, too, this inner warmth was different and strange to him, it had come because of Barton. It was a thought he could not yet cope with.

Twenty-four hours ago he had been asleep across two wooden chairs, on a boat in the English Channel. It seemed years away, he had been another person. How often was he going to feel like that? He almost said his own name out loud, into the quiet orchard, as some kind of reassurance. 'John George Glover Hilliard. Born 10 April 1894. Only son of George Alfred and Constance Hilliard, of Cliff House, Hawton, Sussex, England.'

He remembered the clear, black lettering on the label of the valise in the apple loft.

'What's your name?'

Barton rolled over lazily. 'David.' He had answered at once, because it did not seem an unusual question, though it was, for Hilliard knew the Christian names of very few of the officers here, and would not have thought to ask. He had no occasion to use them, and more, the question would have been regarded as an impertinence. For that matter, he himself might have reacted in the same way. Yet he had said, 'What's your name?' to Barton. He was glad to have done so, glad he knew.

'Had we better be getting back?'

'I suppose so, yes.'

But for some time neither of them made a move.

'I imagine it was fairly painful?'

Hilliard glanced up, startled. Barton was looking with interest at the red, rough-edged scar along his left thigh. It made him want to conceal it hurriedly, he felt ashamed in some odd way, it seemed a blemish, a flaw, for which he was accountable. The only people to look at it until now had been the doctors, and that was not the same thing. He himself had examined it, peering at it closely as he used to peer at scabs and bruises on arms and knees when he was a small boy, charting their progress from blue to brown to yellow, watching the thickening of the skin. He touched this shrapnel wound with the pads of his fingers, sitting on his bed at Hawton, and now Barton was looking at it with the same kind of curiosity.

'You'll see a lot worse than this,' Hilliard said shortly, reaching for his pyjamas.

'But that's not the point, is it? I've never seen any shrapnel wound before, this is the first.'

'You must have seen plenty of gore in your father's surgery.'

'That was different. Isn't this different, for you? It's your own injury, that's the one you know about, that's the one that counts. Only by that can you assess what other people suffer, surely. By the damage to your own flesh, by the amount of pain *you* feel.'

Hilliard thought, how does he know?

'What happened?'

'Not sure. Some bit of metal flying through the air.'

'Oh come!' Barton was laughing at him. 'How *did* it happen?'

'I've told you, I really don't remember too clearly. One minute I was making my way along the trench, trying to get past a pile of pit props someone had left in the way – it was pitch dark – then a shell dropped somewhere behind us and it was a bit flying off that caught my leg. Nobody else was hurt. It all happens so quickly.'

'Just like that?'

'Most of it comes about just like that.' Hilliard snapped his fingers. He thought of the deaths and injuries he had seen, not in battle but caused by the single, random bullet, by a careless accident, by sheer bad luck. One shell coming out of nowhere, through the blue sky of a May morning, singing down into a corner of a trench where Higgins was frying bacon and talking to a couple of men from Glazier's platoon. All killed. Then nothing more that day, only the warm sunshine and ordinary jobs. Sergeant Carson had had his arms blown off demonstrating a new type of hand grenade at the Training Camp. So many pointless, messy, inglorious deaths, 'just like that.' He resented them more than anything.

'Will it disturb you if I keep the lamp on for a bit?'

Hilliard smiled. 'I can sleep through most things.' And so will you, he thought, glancing across to where Barton lay reading *The Turn of the Screw,* propped on his elbow.

'Oh, God …' He spoke before he could stop himself.

'What?' Barton laid down the book at once. 'What's up?'

The last time he had lain in bed like this and looked sideways at the man beside him had been the night before he was sent home from the hospital, the night Crawford had gone away, without giving him anything to help him sleep, so that he had had to lie and hear the noises, look at the rows of humped shapes and feel the pain in his own leg, like a deep burn. Then, the Field-Gunner had stopped crying and spoken suddenly across the space between their beds, half-delirious, had begged Hilliard to talk to him, to help him, help him, to take him away.

'Who are you?' he had said. His face could not be imagined beneath the white bandages. 'I don't know ... Please ... what time is it? What time is it?'

'Just after twelve.'

'Is it day?'

'No.'

'Where is it?'

'This is the hospital.'

'No, no, where is it?'

Uselessly, he had said, 'Shall I get the nurse to come?'

But the Field-Gunner seemed not to hear, he lay muttering words Hilliard could not catch, except now and then a fragment about 'the green light, the green light'. Then, for a few moments, he had surfaced, his voice became clear and quite steady. He said, 'Who are you?'

'Hilliard.'

'Artillery?'

'No, I'm an infantry lieutenant. Look, you'd better get some sleep now, hadn't you? If you can. I don't think you ought to talk.' He turned over himself.

The reply had come out high and urgent, half a cry. 'Oh God, don't go away, talk to me. They keep going away. Don't you go. Please, talk to me, *talk to me.*'

Hilliard could not. He knew that he should have got out of his own bed and sat on the chair beside the Gunner, touched him, given him a drink, let the man know that he would stay there, would listen to whatever it was he had to say, to the incoherent words about the green light. He could not do it, he was too afraid. He had rung the bell and after a long time one of the nurses came, hurrying because they were busy that night, seven men had just been brought in, the survivors from an underground explosion near Artois, she had no time to sit with the Field-Gunner.

'Try and keep him quiet. You can do as much for him as I can, just at the moment.'

Her footsteps went away. The Field-Gunner began to cry again very quietly, as though he had given up hope.

Remembering it now, Hilliard's stomach seemed to come up into his mouth, he thought, 'I fail people.' He did not know what had happened to the Gunner, and it would be impossible to find out. He could not forget the sound of his voice and the sound of his crying.

He got out of bed again, rinsed the tumbler and drank some water. It was lukewarm. Barton was still watching him.

'Hilliard?'

'It's all right.'

'Tell me what's up.'

But he had told him too much already. Barton would have enough of his own to cope with as soon as they left here. He must manage by himself over this, as he had managed in the past.

'Wouldn't it be a good thing for you to talk about it?'

It was not simply what Barton said but his tone of voice, the chance it offered. With shock Hilliard realized that he wanted to cry out as the Field-Gunner had cried, to go across the room to Barton, who would listen, would *know*, as Beth had known on the nights he had crept into her room and slept in the safe darkness beneath her bed.

The surface of his skin went hot as he took in what he had been thinking. Barton had released some anxiety which had been coiled up within him, and there he was now, on the other side of the apple loft, this new person, a stranger, entirely familiar, just as he had been when sitting in the orchard and at the officers' dining table. He was ... What?

Behind him, Barton got out of bed. He went over to one of his cases, opened it and took something out, came back and removed the tumbler from Hilliard's hand. 'Not too much,' he said, 'but it's what you need, I think.' His father might have spoken like that to a patient.

'Go on.'

Hilliard lifted the tumbler. The brandy was slightly diluted by the water which had been left there and it tasted warm and comforting as some medicine of childhood. He drank it slowly.

He remembered the change that came over the men's faces in the cold early mornings as they drank their rum issue, and the colour came seeping back into the night-time greyness and tiredness of the flesh.

'We'd better get some sleep now. They seem to wake up pretty damned early here.'

'When we …' But Hilliard did not go on, he was over-come with such tiredness that he wondered if he could reach his camp-bed. He had been going to say, 'When we get back to the line.' The mornings would be even earlier then and the sleep they had had at night even less. But he would not speak about it after all, there was no point.

His last thought after the lamp had gone out was that he did not want Barton to go up to the front line, he wanted to have him stay behind here, put into some administra-tive job, anything. For he should not be there among the roaring, blasting guns, in such appalling danger, risking his life in the small daily accidents. He thought, we need him, we need what he has to give us. I *need him*.

For the second night he slept without dreaming.

'Any time now.'

'Day after tomorrow.'

'End of this week.'

'Well, it can't last, can it?'

Every day Hilliard heard one man or another prophesy-ing the Battalion's return to the front line. But no order came through, they stayed on at Percelle and after a time, in the September days, that seemed almost as hot as those of June and July, a vague air of restlessness hung about the camp. The men were on edge, wanting to know something for certain. Nothing was said.

The days were taken up with a succession of drills and parades and inspections, lectures, exercises, demonstrations, physical training, bayonet and trench mortar practices. Many of them were resented simply because of their uselessness. Nothing, Hilliard thought, had ever really been taught him which was a true preparation for the everyday physical life of the trenches, no battle went in practice as it went on paper, and so there was no chance to utilize this or that theory. So much of what they had to do here, shocked as they still were, was fatiguing and pointless.

At night the men sat about smoking, playing cards, writing letters in copy-pencil and going over and over again all their stories of that summer, as if they could not help probing a sore. The new recruits listened, their expressions faintly incredulous, as though they were hearing the adventures of old men, for it was so easy here, among the drooping orchards in the sun, it was all an exercise, tedious but unreal, they could not fully imagine what the others talked about.

But, gradually, the faces of those who had been in France through the summer looked less tired and drained, even than when Hilliard had returned, rest and release from immediate fear, and the leave some of them had had, were like moisture, pulping out dehydrated flesh. They were all sunburned.

Only the C.O. was the same, looked haunted, his eyes and hands continually restless. He sent for Hilliard and talked to him, kept Barton telling one story after another over the dinner table, like a child spinning out the time before having to go to bed.

The early mornings were beautiful, when the orchard trees and beyond them those of the copse and the poplars lining the canal loomed as milky shadows out of a thick mist, until the sun struck down, catching the dew on cobwebs, the air cleared. All around Percelle the life of some of the farmers continued, the soldiers met them coming down the lane from the fields, wearing old corduroy trousers and huge shoes. That spring they had almost all been driven away, Percelle had been in a belt of land that had come under a short spell of heavy cross-fire. But the war had moved on far enough for some return to be made to everyday life, though not to normality, for the army and the shattered houses were still there. It was the older people who came back and carried on.

Five miles southwards, the small town of Crevify had escaped much damage, the café tables still stood out on the pavements in the market square, covered in stiff cloths, coffee was served with hot croissants and meringues and éclairs, and in the evenings, bad beer and wine but good brandy. Hilliard and Barton walked there through the fields and, once, the town band came out and played – selections from musical comedies of the nineties, Russian waltzes and French marches, with the late evening sun glittering on their instruments and ruddying the puffed-out faces of the players. Barton sat back, his legs up on another cane chair, smiling with pleasure at the incongruity of it. He said, as Hilliard had said that first evening to Coulter, 'Where's the war?' But the streets of the town were full of their own Battalion, and the only Frenchmen in Crevify were old.

That was the evening when Captain Franklin had gone walking past alone, and Barton had called out to him cheerfully, 'Come and have a drink, sir. Listen to the band!'

For although there was something about the Adjutant which Hilliard did not like, Barton would never agree with him. 'He's all right,' he said, as he said about everyone.

Franklin had stopped and looked across at them, the same lack of expression on his long face. His skin was not tanned but reddened by the sun.

'The beer's rotten but the chairs are comfortable.'

Hilliard had not thought that anyone in the world could have resisted Barton's friendliness, the knack he had of attracting all available company. Franklin did not move, but there had been something like disapproval on his face, though in fact he had not looked at Barton but at Hilliard when he spoke. 'I won't if you don't mind. I'm on my way back.' And walked on slowly. But when Hilliard swore, Barton had only said, 'Oh, he's all right!' as always and then forgot it calling for more drinks.

It was here at the café table that he wrote so many of his letters. Because, for every one Hilliard sent, his friend wrote four or five, long letters in quick, black handwriting, sprinkled with exclamation marks and, when he was writing to his sisters, with small drawings and doodles in the margins, for their children.

'What do you find *to say?*' Hilliard had once asked, watching the flow of Barton's hand on and on, page after page. He had looked up, puzzled.

'Oh, there's no shortage of material, surely?'

'Isn't there?'

'I tell them what we do all day, I describe this place, what I can see, who goes by, what the band's playing, and then there are all the questions to answer and ask – oh, we have jokes and so forth.'

'Jokes?'

'Family jokes – you know the kind of thing.'

Hilliard did not. His own letters to his family – and he wrote to them collectively, now that he had nothing private left to say to Beth – were dull, full of polite thanks for parcels and always, when he read them over, very much the same. He never referred to Barton.

'When the war's over or we manage to hit leave at the same time you can come and meet them all,' Barton had said. 'Then you'll know who I'm talking about and writing to, you'll get them sorted out.'

Though Hilliard had imagined them endlessly, these people who shared so much with Barton, he had looked at their faces, staring out at him from the photographs, and put names to them and remembered their individual characteristics, as Barton had described them, he built up the family piece by piece within his own mind. It pleased him.

He said, 'I wouldn't much like you to meet my family.'

'Oh, I think we'd probably get on rather well.'

'No.'

'Why? I get along with most people.'

Yes, that was true, and he saw at once that Barton would charm his mother and tease Beth, would listen to his father without impatience, would take trouble over the Major, and that they would all like him. But he wanted to keep Barton to himself.

Then, Barton's mother had sent him a message. It came at the end of one of her long letters. 'And all kind thoughts to your nice friend John Hilliard.'

Barton had read it out mockingly. 'You're my "nice friend" – there now!'

Hilliard felt both acute pleasure and, again, a curious unease. He was afraid, too, of being known and referred to by this person he had never seen, by Barton's mother, whose name was Miriam and wore her hair in a soft loose bun at the nape of her neck, whose features were both plain and pretty and also strangely old-fashioned. Hilliard could not imagine his own mother sending any messages to a young man she had never met even making allowances for the informalities of wartime. He had only managed to say, 'Oh – well, thank her very much.'

'Right.'

And he had watched Barton's hand move smoothly across the paper, seen the words form upside down. 'Hilliard says, "thank you very much"!!!'

The message back in the next letter had been, 'John Hilliard is clearly a man of few words.'

'So you'll have to do better next time,' Barton had said.

He gave Hilliard most of his letters to read, sharing them with as little concern as Hilliard shared the Fortnum and Mason's groceries in his parcels.

After that a dialogue was established between him and the Barton family, mother and father, brothers and sisters, short messages were passed, jokes made and he was at first uncertain how to manage it all, for he had never experienced such people. But when he said as much, Barton looked amused and only said, 'Well, you have now!' Hilliard knew that he did not completely understand, for to him his own family were the norm, were altogether known and presented no problems. Besides, people never did present problems to him, he got along, as he said, with everyone.

'I hope we keep Mr Barton with us, sir,' Coulter said, coming up into the apple loft one afternoon when Hilliard was changing into his riding boots. 'He's done the world of good to this company, anyone can see that He's done the C.O. good as well, sir.'

'You're right, yes.'

'You know what happens though, sir – we always lose our best officers.' Then, turning and catching sight of Hilliard's expression, he added, 'No, sir, what I mean is, they ship them off to another Battalion or put them up at Brigade H.Q. just when we need them. You know that, sir – how they mess us about, and it's never the ones we could do without, is it?'

'Well, let's hope it doesn't happen.'

'Yes, sir. By the way, sir, I don't know if anything's up but I hear the Brigadier's coming down tomorrow.'

'Probably just routine.'

'Checking up on us, yes, sir.'

'I suppose we'd better get some rifle cleaning done though – give him something to approve of!'

'If you ask me, sir, the men are all a bit sick of rifle cleaning and such, they've cleaned them till they're about worn away, this past week or so.'

'I know. But do you think they'd rather be on the move?'

But the Brigadier's visit passed off quickly and without event, the men waited all the rest of that day and on into the evening, for some order. None came. It was only Hilliard who was sent for by Garrett – Garrett, who looked more than ever anxious, as though this long rest period were getting on his nerves, too, he would rather move back up and have it over with.

He said, 'Captain Franklin thinks one of B Company might go off on a gas course. He thinks it would be useful. I've told him I didn't want to spare you, Hilliard. If we get our marching orders this week I want you with your platoon. There are few enough experienced officers left in this Battalion, God knows. But Franklin's got some bee in his bonnet about it. I said I'd have a word with you. Perhaps we'd better send Barton? That's what Franklin had in mind.'

'How long would it last?'

'A week plus a couple of days' travelling.'

'Are you asking for my opinion, sir?'

'I suppose so.' Garrett shifted the papers about on his desk. 'Yes. Opinion. Advice. I don't know.'

'We're not likely to stay here much longer, are we? We can't possibly.'

Garrett was silent.

'Well – you probably don't know anything about it, but that much does seem obvious. We don't get an indefinite rest period and we've overstayed this one, surely? So the chances are that we'll be going somewhere or other within a day or two. And – I would rather Barton stayed and went with us. I think …' He paused. Garrett was staring down at the table, perhaps not even listening.

'I think we need him.'

'Yes.' A bluebottle droned on and on against the window pane, behind the desk. For a long time, Garrett sat, mesmerized. Hilliard noticed the faint, brown discolorations on the backs of his hands, like the mottling on the skin of a much older man. Garrett was not fifty. 'Yes, I know.' He looked up and into Hilliard's face. 'Only Franklin seems to …'

What? Garrett did not finish. Then, Hilliard knew for certain that the Adjutant disliked both Barton and himself, distrusted them, perhaps, and had done so for no good reason, from the beginning, from the first night at the dining table when he had not smiled at Barton's stories about his horse-riding Aunt Eustacia.

'Well – I'll think about it. I can't decide just now. I thought I'd find out how you saw it, that was all.'

Hilliard went out of the room and through the low

doorway into the yard. The farm dog came bounding across from between the trees, nuzzling at his legs, as he nuzzled those of anyone who stopped for a moment in his vicinity. Hilliard roughed the hair of its head automatically. Franklin wanted Barton to go. Perhaps the gas course was only the first move in some plan to get him permanently transferred. Well, had he himself not wished, every day now, that Barton should not have to go up to the front line?

The sun dipped down between the trees of the copse and for a second or two flamed straight into his face.

He did not want Barton to go away.

'Franklin won't be pleased.'

'What the hell?' Barton lay on his bed reading a letter. The C.O. had sent someone else on the gas course.

'Only that it's better to get on with your senior officers if at all possible. It makes life easier.'

'Life seems perfectly all right to me.'

For the first time, Hilliard lost his temper. 'Don't be so bloody complacent. You haven't been anywhere yet, you haven't seen anything. You're in a *rest camp,* remember? You don't know what you're talking about but you damn soon will.'

'I know,' Barton said quietly.

Hilliard was silent.

'Look, I don't really care for Franklin much more than you do, John, but it's a perfectly irrational dislike. He's done nothing to me at all – or to you, for that matter. It's a pure case of Dr Fell.'

'Oh, no. He's got it in for us.'

'Why?'

'I've no idea.'

'If it boils down to it, he doesn't seem to like anyone much, does he?' Barton sat up and swung his legs over the side of the bed. 'He doesn't have any particular friends, doesn't do much in the way of relaxation except play bridge, and even then, it's for the sake of the game, not the company.'

'He doesn't like to see other people being friendly.'

'Nonsense. He could perfectly well have friends himself if he chose. He wouldn't have to put himself out a great deal, but he doesn't choose.'

'Why?'

'Lord, Hilliard, *I* don't know.'

'A Captain is easily capable of making one's life a misery at the front, if he has half a mind.'

'I should have thought that went for a C.O. or a Brigadier or for that matter for one's own batman.'

'All the same …'

'Oh, forget it, forget it.' Barton laid a hand on his shoulder, laughing. 'I didn't go on the gas course, about which I'm fairly relieved. I didn't enjoy all that plunging in and out of smoke-filled chambers at the Training Camp. I never could bear masks over my face. Franklin didn't get his way. Now, let's make the most of this place, while we can.'

Footsteps came quickly up the ladder. Whenever Coulter appeared, Hilliard could imagine him in the circus ring, he half-expected him to take a leap off the floor of the loft on to some trapeze dangling from a beam. He had given them an off-the-cuff juggling display one afternoon in the mess kitchen, throwing spinning saucers up into the air, and balancing glasses of water on his nose; 'What are you doing in the army, Coulter? You should have stayed on at home and kept their spirits up!'

Coulter brought the crockery down neatly, piece by piece, turned and began to stack it away. 'I'm right out of practice, sir, if you did but know it. Besides, I joined up to come to France, didn't I, this is where the war is. I'm more use here than in a circus ring just at present.' For Coulter was aggressive about the war, still patriotic and still confident, in spite of all he had seen. He had a distant respect for the Generals, close admiration for the officers of his own regiment. It was only politicians about whom he might occasionally say a bad word. But Hilliard liked Coulter, he had come to rely on him, though their relationship was entirely different from the one he had had with his former batman, the morose Bates. Coulter was more easygoing, he had greater nerve, and probably less stamina. But no, you couldn't say that, for it was impossible to tell until you were in the line, you couldn't pass any kind of true judgement upon a man, here, in the uneasy calm and quiet of the rest camp.

Now, Coulter did not come into the loft, only to put his head through the hatchway. 'Excuse me, sir – the C.O. wants to see both of you right away, sir. He wants to see all the officers. It seems as if there's something up.'

Garrett looked calmer, full of some sort of relief. The Battalion was leaving Percelle first thing the next morning for

the front lines at Lully, near Barmelle Wood and Queronne, an area which had been under heavy fire for the past
six or seven weeks.

For the rest of that day the atmosphere of the farm
changed, and the yard and the orchard and the lane
leading down from the village were full of men moving
about shouting orders, carts arrived, two advance motor
buses came, were packed up, left again. The farm dog wandered about and was repeatedly pushed out of the way,
until it retired behind the stables.

Hilliard thought that the men were relieved, as Garrett
had been, no matter what might be to come: they knew
where they were now, were able to immerse themselves in
physical activity with a clear end in view.

He noticed that Franklin was everywhere, supervising
everything, though he seemed to be in no hurry and his
face showed no interest in what went on. He would be
a good officer under fire, efficient and cool-headed. But
Hilliard disliked him more than ever.

Garrett had ordered the evening meal to be put back
by an hour because there was so much to be done, they
would not be eating in the officers' mess until after nine.
But Hilliard's platoon had finished earlier, there were only
the tents and kit-bags to be put up just before they set off
the following morning.

He found Barton.

'I'd like to walk down to the orchard.'

'Say a fond farewell!'

'Why not?'

'Indeed.'

'Hilliard?'

They both turned. Hilliard walked back towards where the Adjutant was standing, outside the stables.

'Either you or Barton will have to be on foot tomorrow. There aren't enough horses for everyone.'

'Harrison's gone off on that gas course, though.'

'There still aren't enough, too many are needed for carrying.'

'I see. Well, Barton had better ride in that case, sir.'

'I'd prefer it if you did. You know the form, you can keep an eye on things. We'll probably be stopping overnight at Feuvry.'

'Yes.'

'All right.' Franklin turned and strolled back towards the farmhouse.

But when Hilliard told him, full of annoyance, Barton only smiled. 'I don't mind marching. I'd prefer it, actually. I did walk 800 miles down through Italy with my brother a couple of years ago, you know.'

'That's not the point.'

'Ah!'

'He could perfectly well have asked someone else.'

'But he didn't, that's all there is to it.'

'He's making bloody sure we don't waste time tomorrow chatting together.'

'Don't be so touchy – you've got a thing about this. And would we, in any case? We'd both have too much else to do and we know it and Franklin knows it.'

Hilliard let out a long breath. 'You're too good natured,' he said. 'I ought to be more like you.'

'Perhaps I just plump for a quiet life.'

'No.'

He looked at Barton, walking beside him with his odd, loose gait. The Battalion barber had shorn him up the back of the neck but he had not managed to prevent the front hair from falling. In a thick ledge over his forehead, so that he looked as though he held his head at an angle, that the front might suddenly tip, unbalancing him.

'Well,' Barton said. It was simply an expression of contentment.

They had come through the copse into the orchard, and were following the bank of the stream. The sky was mulberry coloured, over the church.

Barton stopped. 'I can smell something.'

There were no sounds except the song of larks and blackbirds and the trickle of water over flint-stones.

'Can't you smell it?'

'Burning? Yes, I can now.'

They looked around the orchard, nothing.

'It's probably the camp kitchen.'

'We're too far away and there's no wind. Besides, it's a different sort of smell.'

'I can't see anything. I suppose the farmers must burn things. It's autumn – bonfire time.'

They moved on. The stream flowed under a small wooden footbridge and then curved away slightly. If they were not going to be late, they ought to turn back here.

'I can still smell it,' Barton said. Then they both caught sight of the fine line of smoke, rising from behind the sycamore copse, a hundred yards or so ahead, nearer the church.

'It is a bonfire.'

'No.'

Barton began to run, his legs covering the ground remarkably quickly, so that Hilliard was well behind, going through the thick grass. He heard a shout.

As far as they knew nobody had seen or heard the plane come down. Indeed, there had been very few planes over this area at all during the past few weeks and when one did appear it had seemed unreal, a distant reminder of war.

This one, a small German monoplane, had smashed nose forward into the field immediately behind the copse. It was badly charred at the front, like some ungainly bird which had been half shoved into an oven. The smoke was dying away, the plane might have been here since early that morning.

'What do we do?'

'Go back and report it. Though one of the farmers probably has already. But we'll have to check.'

It looked an ugly plane. They were about to turn away.

'Good God,' Barton said. He had gone much closer and now he stopped. Hilliard moved up to his side.

The pilot was still strapped into his seat but he had slid forward and down. His head was bent over to one side and the eyes were open, looking over in the direction of the trees. He had a plump, young face, with high cheekbones, and the flesh of it was quite undamaged. His front teeth protruded slightly, to rest on the bottom lip. But Hilliard saw that the rest of his body, up to the chest and arms, was almost burned away. He wondered why the plane had not gone up in flames completely and, as it had not, why the man could not have scrambled out.

'We shall have to report it,' he said. He had a sudden feeling of acute reality, he was back, now, in the world where such things happened, were normal. This was the first dead man he had seen since his return to France and there would now only be all the rest who were to follow. He felt the old, heavy sensation in his stomach, misery and fear and anger, compounded but also slightly deadened.

But he was used to it. Barton was not. Glancing at his face now, Hilliard recognized in another what he himself had known, the first time he saw a corpse in France. There were only a limited number of responses he could make. He remembered the one that the Sergeant who was leading him up the trench they called Pall Mall had made, when they came upon a heap of perhaps forty bodies piled up together, bloated and black, unburied for weeks, for this part of the line had been particularly bad, there had been a large number of casualties and no time to do anything about them.

He had said, 'Mind your feet, sir.'

Perhaps Barton was being broken in gently, after all. He did not look as if he thought so. His face had not gone paler but more darkly flushed under the already sunburned skin; he said nothing. Hilliard thought that he would do anything now, anything at all, for him not to have to go, not to see any more of it: he was almost beside himself in a rush of dread on Barton's behalf.

It had gone much darker, the birds were quiet. The smoke still plumed up from the engine of the German plane, there was the faint tick-tack of cooling metal.

'Come on.' Barton jerked his head up. 'We'd better go back.'

'David …'

Barton stopped, glanced back. He said, 'No. It's all right.'

They both began to run.

Much later, in the apple loft, where all their things stood about in cases and bags, waiting to be moved, he said, 'Pity, I shan't be able to think about it in the same way now. I shan't remember the orchard without remembering that bloody plane.'

'I suppose we shouldn't have gone back for a last look. It's generally a mistake, isn't it?'

'Oh, no,' Barton turned the lamp down. 'After all, it had to start somewhere, didn't it?'

PART TWO

'Mounted officers should avoid passing and re-passing infantry more than is absolutely necessary,'

And so they *had* only seen one another twice that day, at the second halt early in the morning and then as the Battalion was going into Feuvry, and Hilliard happened to ride by. He had passed Barton and then glanced back over his shoulder, seen his expression and frowned. Barton knew at once what he thought. John saw that he was more affected by the sight of this town than he had been by the dead German pilot in the burned-out plane, and he was shocked.

But until then he had enjoyed the march from Percelle, though it had taken him a long time, more than an hour, to relax, in his position behind B Company, for he was anxious in case he should overlook anything for which he was responsible, in case, through his fault, something went wrong.

The hard feeling of the road under his feet pleased him and he did not mind that it was hot and dry, with the line of the horizon shimmering and shifting ahead. He had spent so much of his life walking. The year before he left school he had gone with his younger brother to the Camargue, they had taken tents and lived on bread and cheese and walked for miles every day over that flat, pale, sinister countryside.

He enjoyed the sight of the men moving together, enjoyed the sound of their singing.

'The men are lucky,' Hilliard had said, 'in some ways they're better off than we are. In some ways, I envy them.'

'What do you envy?'

'They get along, they have one another the whole time. They're all friends. Don't you notice that? It's easier. They just get along.'

'Don't we?'

'It isn't the same.' Hilliard had hesitated, unable to explain, that this friendship of theirs, so immediately, simply achieved, was rare, could not be taken for granted, or seen elsewhere. Among the officers there was not the natural camaraderie to be found among the men. They had so much work to do individually.

The men were singing.

Captain Sparrow
Captain Sparrow
From Harrow
on the Hill,
We've got him with us still
Captain Sparrow.
And he …

Captain Sparrow was riding a long way behind.

'The length of an average march under normal conditions for a large column is fifteen miles a day. INFANTRY USUAL PACE. Yards per minute – 100. Minutes required to traverse one mile – 18. Miles per hour including short halts – 3.'

The sun shone. Later on in the day, when they hit the main road to the front, they found it crowded with horses and motor bicycles and men.

'What is it, Hughins?'

'Only the usual, sir. Blisters. They feel like mushrooms.'

'Oh.' Barton remembered what you did with blisters, how you took off shoe and sock, and burst them carefully or, better still, got someone else to do it for you, and then covered the place up with clean lint. They had always been getting blisters, as children.

Hughins was loosening his boot gingerly, trying to screw the thick sock around inside. For who could sit here at the roadside halt with bare feet, and have his blisters pricked delicately by someone with a clean needle and a steady hand, who had lint to spare?

'Nothing a nice hot mustard soak won't put right when we get to the hotel! And I rub them with rum as well – works wonders, sir.' Hughins seemed old to Barton, old enough to be his father, though he could not be. He was a handsome man, but he had warts on his chin.

'Well – let me know if they get any worse.'

'Oh yes, sir, I'll shout. I could do with a nice week in hospital. Or even a ride on a horse!'

They lay on their backs and their faces burned darker than ever in the mid-day sun and their cigarette smoke plumed gently upwards, wavering blue.

ADVANCE!

He enjoyed marching. He did not mind how far they had to go, did not have blisters like Hughins. Did not think ahead. They passed through a village in which people were still living and some girls waved to them from windows.

The men sang.

You would like it here. The autumn has really come now. We passed by a canal and along its bank most of the poplars were quite bare, the water was still and clogged with all the yellow leaves. The splendid thing about marching is, you just have to go. You assume someone else knows exactly where. There's always someone over you who knows more than you do and you're not in any way responsible, so you point yourself in the direction indicated and off you go. Perhaps I'm lucky, having done so much walking in the course of my life already. Anyway, I'm glad of the training, now!

John has to ride today. Though I think he enjoys it – in fact I'm sure he does, and certainly better than I would, I always feel very insecure on the back of a horse. But John rides about and he is tall and has a good seat, he relaxes and looks over the tops of all our heads.

I must say, today I feel like one of the men and he is one of the officers! Still, I'm perfectly happy. I get on well with our platoon. Now the field kitchen is coming up, I shall have to put this away. There are so many butterflies here, the summer has kept them going. John has just gone by, but without a chance of speaking. They are much concerned with watering the horses, in weather like this. Roly would enjoy seeing it all.

'I wouldn't mind having a shilling for every letter you've written since I first met you, Barton.' He had wished, then, for some way of conveying the idea, the knowledge of his family, complete and whole, to John Hilliard, of bestowing it like a nugget, something to be held out in the palm of his hand. There they are, take them! For when he talked about them all, perhaps he got it wrong, perhaps John received no true picture of how it was. Just as he himself could not imagine the coldness in Hilliard's family, the distance that seemed to exist between all of them.

'It's different for you. You find things easier.'

Did he? Yes, he supposed so. Certainly he found this friendship easier, he had accepted it at once, even as he recognized its rarity. It had startled him. He had stood in the apple loft at Percelle and heard the footsteps of the man they had all talked about and who had now come back, Hilliard, whose name had been mentioned in despatches and had been wounded, who was only a year older than he was and about whom the C.O. thought so highly, whose belongings were here in this room he had already come to think of as entirely his own. He had been curious, apprehensive for some reason. *What will he be like?*

Then, John Hilliard's head had appeared in the space at the top of the ladder, the pale hair and the very long neck, he had looked across at Barton, a quick, cautious look. Then at once it had been all right, and more than that. He did not know what. But whatever it was, he took it much more in his stride than John, whose face looked uncertain so often, who glanced at him and then away again quickly, as they were walking. Barton felt the need to reassure him.

'Goodbye, Dolly, I must leave you …'

It is all just as you would imagine it, today, they sing all the right songs. You would hear them and nod and smile to yourself, and fit us into one of your pigeon holes, we are behaving as soldiers in France are all supposed to behave, marching and singing Dolly Grey, though nobody at all sings Tipperary, I have not heard it once since I came out – it seems to be an invention from home. You really *would* like the sight of John riding his horse, that would please you.

'Do you always tell them everything you think and feel? In your letters?'

'Yes,' Barton had said. For why not? What else should he do? What was there to be kept back? John had frowned, unable to understand.

I think you would want me to look as good as he does but I never could. I'm simply a sack of potatoes in a saddle. A little while ago a Troop of Lancers trotted down the road in the opposite direction. We stared like small boys. They looked quite amazing, they glittered in the sun like all the soldiers in all the armies of history, and the feet of their horses made so little noise as they hit the ground. Not like ours, pulling carts and so forth. I wish you could all have seen them.

The countryside began to change. There were fewer valleys and fewer trees and many of them were split by shells. It was drier, with a different kind of dryness. There seemed never to have been any water here at all. The fields were full of old shell craters, and the sides of the roads were covered in white-grey dust from all the passing of carts and horses and motors and men.

B Company were singing verses made up by Fyson

to a hymn tune, and the verses became more obscene and libellous as they went on, until Barton called out a warning, not because he minded but before anyone who did mind should hear them, and for a time after that they marched in silence, their ranks uneven. They were tired. He called to them to close up. He thought they resented him. Hughins was limping.

Behind, some of A Company had taken up 'Dolly Grey'.

They heard the whine and crash of a shell, coming out of nowhere, and the whole column ducked, though they did not stop marching, and the shell was not near. One of the horses had shied into a ditch and was being spurred out. Barton felt suddenly anxious.

They were going towards the town of Feuvry. He could see a pall of reddish dust hanging over the buildings, from shattered bricks and shell.

Memorandum. Commanding Officer to 2nd Battalion:
At Feuvry we shall be in close billets. Guards will be mounted at once. Great precautions must be taken with drinking water and sanitation.

Feuvry had been occupied by the Germans in the summer of 1914, and relieved by the B.E.F. and evacuated – and then shelled ever since, until it was almost derelict. It was disliked, the name of it was disliked by the whole army. A superstition had attached itself to Feuvry. The men groaned, glanced at one another uneasily, hearing that they were to stay there.

But when he had asked about it, Hilliard had shaken his head, for he had never been there himself. So they only knew what they had heard, what the men said. Barton was not sure what to expect. Perhaps something like Percelle on a large scale, red-brick buildings with roofs caved in, crumbling walls already overgrown with convolvulus. He had grown fond of Percelle even as it was, the village looked as though it had tumbled down after years of neglect, rather than been damaged by shell fire.

He was not prepared for Feuvry. As the column marched in and turned down what was left of the main street, going towards a square, Hilliard had ridden close by. Had seen that Barton was appalled by Feuvry, as he had not been by the sight of the dead pilot in the crashed plane.

The men were swaying on their feet, were seeing nothing, were not singing.

Feuvry.

This is a terrible place. How can I describe it to you? How would you ever be able to imagine what I can see? I do not think there is a building left intact and there are many which are just holes in the ground, or piles of rubble. All along the sides of the road, too, there is every kind of rubbish. But you would not have called it that if you had seen it in its original state. I mean, rubbish is not what most of it used to be, apart from the mess of broken brick and girders. These are all things from people's houses. You see a chair, sticking out spring coils from sofas and they are all charred and rusted. There are bedsteads and mattresses and piles of bloodstained clothing, part of a smashed wash-basin, children's toys. And then there is all the litter of the armies, of course. Before us, there were the occupying forces. Everything has been left in the most appalling mess. So much of the rubble is old, two years old, and has never been shifted, so that there are plenty of things you cannot recognize any longer.

Everything smells, reeks, of years of decay and shell-fire and burned wood. I find myself thinking all the time of how it must have been – though really it is hard to reconstruct a town out of all this: and of the people who lived ordinary lives here, who saved up for these things, owned and enjoyed them, and now they all mean nothing, they are rubbish, rolling about in corners, rotting in heaps. We have what they are pleased to call houses for our billets. The men are twenty or thirty to a tiny room, and they are in a bad state, dirty and everything broken. There isn't a whole roof, and scarcely a whole floor. The water supply and all the sanitation system is hopelessly polluted, we have to look for rats everywhere. And then there are so many dead bodies, because the place has been in the direct line of fire for so long. Ambulances come through but they seem to have missed a lot and they only take away the possible survivors, now. They are too hard pressed fetching and carrying the wounded from the front lines.

I came across a man sitting upright in a doorway, with his bayonet fixed, but he was quite dead, he must have been on sentry duty. It was not apparent how he died, he seemed to have no injuries, only some terrible distortion of his face. It was as though he had blown up inside, but nothing had come out. He belonged to a regiment which was here two weeks ago.

The horses are better off than we are, they have gone into stables half a mile away, and we won't have much to do with them from now on, as we go into the trenches straightaway. Well, I'm glad they look after them. As for us – I'm aching a bit but not tired. I cannot stop looking around me and seeing more ugliness and mess than I have seen in my life. John is quiet and a bit tense. He doesn't say much and in any case we're pretty busy. The men are getting rum issue, which they deserve, so I shall have to go and see to it in a moment. It comes up in a gallon jar, and must never be let out of the sight of an officer!

Actually, the men deserve long cool drinks of water even more than rum but it's rationed here, so they get short measure and it tastes of the stuff they use to sterilize it. God knows if we'll ever get a wash. I'm already beginning to feel the squalor of the army at war. My feet have sweated inside my boots and the rest of me inside my uniform. My hair feels dusty and sticky at the same time. Oh, you wouldn't like me at all just now! John would say this is nothing, you wait and see, this is cushy compared to what will come later on. Well, he is probably right. But so often now have I seen him biting back that kind of remark. I suppose he wants to save me from knowing anything before I've absolutely got to. But I've got some imagination and eyes to see and ears to hear, I've a pretty good idea about what's coming and that it won't be anybody's idea of a picnic.

I must say I shall mind being filthy and physically in a mess more than the thing I *thought* I should mind most of all – that is, the having no time or place or scarcely anything to call my own. Because, oddly enough, one does have a fair measure of all those – so far, at any rate. And I am happy being with our platoon, and with John. I don't at all mind the idea that I'm doing this or that along with a few thousand other people. Perhaps that's the advantage of coming from a large family!

But really it isn't at all fair to say what I do or don't mind, I haven't seen much yet except Training Camp and rest camp. Not until today, at least. This place is so frighteningly *ugly*, and the guns are still battering away at it the whole time. They have ruined the church here, which was apparently Romanesque and very beautiful, with a lovely tower. I hadn't realized what a noise the guns make, though they are not really near to us and in fact a lot of it is echo from what buildings are left. I don't care to think about the noise of the guns and shells when I actually come near them. It's the one idea which really does bother me. I have never been very good with loud noises, have I? And it has been so quiet and peaceful at the camp. You wouldn't have known there was anything much going on at all for a hundred miles. Some days I might have been at home, sitting down by the beck. Well, it's going to be different for some while now.

I think I should like some fruit in a parcel, please, especially if we are going to continue to be rationed with our water. Apples or oranges would be nice. You will know what travels well, better than I do, as it takes a while for parcels to reach us. And longer now, I imagine. But here's the Sergeant with the rum jar ...

'What are you doing?'
'Finishing a letter.'
'Tell me, did you manage to get a dozen or two written while you were actually marching?'
'Certainly!'
They were in the tiny back washroom of what had once been a tall, perhaps even rather stylish house – the wallpaper which was left was elaborate and expensive-looking. Now, the windows were boarded up, and the basin had gone: above their heads, the plaster and wood of the ceiling sagged down and when the guns vibrated they were showered with flakes and splinters. The room smelled stuffy, with the grease from their candle and with old dirt and dust. There was nothing in it at all, apart from what they themselves had brought except for an old stone flower-urn, ornate and quite undamaged, with a little, greenish soil still in the bottom.

It was late by the time they had seen Garrett, who was across the street in what had been a school. The cupboards hung open and, inside on the shelves, books were piled up, bundled with string and covered in dust. Names were written in pencil on the plaster at desk level: Genevieve Maury. Marie Crêpes. Jean Bontin. Adèle P.

Barton wondered where they all were.

Coming back, a shell had soared over their heads and they had raced for a doorway. Barton's head and limbs were aching now. His eyes smarted, in the smoke from the candle.

'For heaven's sake …'

'Ah right. Sorry.'

He had just written:

There is something all the men hate about this place. Now, I can sense it myself. Something old and bad and dead, a smell, a feeling you get as you walk across the street. It is not simply the bodies lying all about us, and the fact that the guns are firing, it is something else, something …

Hilliard had pulled his blanket half over him. Barton put the letter away. Footsteps on the stairs. None of the rooms in this house had doors.

'Sir?'

Hilliard sat up at once. 'What is it?'

'I'd be glad if you could come, sir. It's Harris.' The Sergeant was invisible in the doorway. His voice sounded both apologetic and urgent. Hilliard was pushing off his blanket.

'Let me go,' Barton was on his feet. 'You've been at it since we got here. You'd far better get some sleep.'

For he had seen John trying to work himself into a state of exhaustion, his face had been pale and stiff, and Barton had realized that he'd had time to think all day, riding the horse, going back to the front, remembering. There had been no marching to tire out his body.

'I'll go.'

Besides, if there was something wrong, he felt in a mood to be at the centre of it, to see at once how bad everything could be. He was not tired, in spite of the physical aching. But Hilliard was behind him.

'Harris?'

'Yes, sir.'

'Where is he?'

'He's gone down into the cellar, sir. We're not using it – but he's in a bit of a state.'

They were going away.

'You'd better stay here, Barton.'

He lit the candle again and watched the light flicker yellow through a gap in the ceiling. It was perfectly correct, John was in charge of the platoon, it was his job to go. All the same he resented it. 'You'd better stay here.' He had wanted to take charge. The idea was new to him and he thought about it, for he was not ambitious, did not want to lead, he had been perfectly content, *was* content. He had no illusions about himself as actual or potential soldier, no convictions about his duty in this war, no real desire to be here at all; except that he would not want to leave Hilliard, now. Yet he had wanted to go behind Sergeant Locke, down the stairs, to be responsible.

He reached over to his tunic for the letter and pencil.

I'll send this off tomorrow, before we leave here. It's very late now, but ...

The room was filled with greenish light for a second, and then there was a whine and the crash of an exploding shell. He had no idea how close it had been but nothing had come as near as that before.

Now, it was quite dark again. He seemed to be all right. Much further away, guns boomed – a different sound.

'Are you all right?' Hilliard was in the doorway.

'Perfectly, thanks. The candle went out.'

'Do you think you could come down.'

'What's happened?'

'Nothing – not really. It's Harris.'

'Yes?'

'I can't get him to move. Nobody can. The men have tried, I've said what I can think of, but he isn't ... he's taken himself down there and he won't come out. He doesn't seem to hear us at all.'

'What's he doing?'

'Nothing. He's in a corner. He's been there for a couple of hours apparently. They've been trying to persuade him to come out.'

'Is he ill?'

'I don't think so. He won't say anything.'

'Can't he be left there?'

'Not in his present state, no. And he'll have to come out in the morning. I shall have to get Franklin if he won't budge for us.'

'No. We'll cope.'

They made their way down the unsteady staircase and along the passages of the house. Around them in the darkness the men lay, sleeping or listening. They picked their way between the blankets. Down in what had been the kitchen, the floor was stone and there were neither doors, windows, nor boards at the gaps. There was the whine of another shell and the sound of bricks crashing down, somewhere in the north of the town.

The other men of the platoon who had tried to help had now been sent away, only Sergeant Locke stood in the cellar, holding a candle. It smelled down here, a fouler smell, there might once have been latrines or rats. A stone ledge was let into the far wall, like a fireplace but without any chimney leading up from it. Harris was huddled inside like a foetus, his hands up near his face. He was not moving but making a continuous, agonized noise, a cry or a moan and yet neither of those. Barton remembered watching him play football in the orchard at Percelle. He was perhaps eighteen, stocky and red-headed. He had a harmonica, which he used to accompany their songs in the evening.

'I thought you might know what to say to him better than I do.'

For a moment the three of them stood in the small pool of light in the dank cellar, looking towards the soldier, hearing him. The guns roared again and the boy's voice rose a pitch higher. Barton remembered that Harris had come to the camp on the same train as Hilliard. Had taken scraps across the yard to the farm dog, each evening.

'It might be better if I stayed with him on my own for a bit, mightn't it?'

They hesitated.

'If you can get him to go back upstairs, sir, he'll calm down, he'll be all right when he's with the others again, they'll see to him. If we can get him out of here.'

'Yes,' Hilliard said. 'It's no use crowding in on him, you're quite right. I'll go back. Call me if you want help. Sergeant will you wait at the top of the stairs?'

'Sir.'

Barton nodded. 'I'll bring him up.' Hilliard's face relaxed. They went away, out of the cellar and up the steps, to the noise of the guns in the distance.

Oh God, he is two years younger than me, he is Edward's age, he knows no more about it than I do, we have neither of us seen anything, only heard, only heard. We can imagine it, that's all. And I have to tell him that he must get up and go back, must pull himself together, and that tomorrow he must march on with the rest of us. In the end, he has to be ordered to do that.

He went forward quietly. The cellar floor was uneven. He stopped close beside the ledge, set down the candle. He could see Harris's face, strangely altered with fear. He wondered how it would be with him when they got to the front line and into the trenches and into battle.

He put out his hand and found Harris's wrist and held it. He remembered the time when he had fallen out of a willow tree near the beck and lain on the ground and seen his own blood and cried out from fear at the sight, and

Edward had held his wrist like that then, though he too had been afraid of the blood. Nevertheless, it had comforted them both.

For a moment the noise went on, the terrible, high moan. Harris's pulse was thudding. Barton did not move his hand. He said, 'I'll stay here. It's all right.'

He wondered what Captain Franklin would have done.

In a pause from the sound of the shelling, he heard a man bumping as he turned over on the floor overhead.

'Harris?'

The boy's teeth began to chatter. The skin of his wrist felt hot under Barton's touch. For a long time neither of them moved. Then Harris lurched up, and forwards, his head touched his knees and he began to cry, not lifting his hands to wipe his face. Barton waited. The crying went on and on. Then, quite abruptly, stopped.

'I can't go,' Harris said. Whispered. He looked up into Barton's face. 'I'm afraid.'

'Yes.'

He wanted to weep, then, he felt old, he thought that he had seen and heard all that he ever needed to see, all the fear there could be, that he, too, could not go.

You wait, you don't know anything, you haven't seen anything yet, Barton. You wait.

Now, he had. And they were only here in Feuvry, three miles or more away from the front line. Only here.

'What'll happen to me, sir? What'll happen to me? I can't go.'

Barton stayed in the cellar for a long time with Harris, patiently hearing the tale of misery and fear, and there was nothing he could do about any of it, he was distressed at his own inadequacy, there was none of it that he had not felt or imagined himself. Harris had spent much of his time at Percelle listening to the stories all the men had been telling about that summer's offensive, the tales of death and horror had lodged in his mind and bred fear, until today, after the march and the heat and his tiredness, he had broken under the strain of them.

But in the end, somehow, Barton got him to come out, to agree that he must go back upstairs among the others, for then nothing would be said or done to him, and that, tomorrow, he would march on again, up to the front line.

He heard his own words and they echoed in his ears and he wondered at them, for they were meaningless, false, they gave him no comfort – how, then, could they do anything for Harris? He was only certain that Franklin must not have to be informed. He said as much.

'You do see that it would be better not, don't you?'

Silence. Then, 'Yes, sir.'

'If you come up now, it'll all be forgotten.'

'Sergeant Locke …'

'Won't say anything.'

'I'm …'

Silence again for a long time. Harris still had his knees hunched up to his chest. It was dark in the cellar now, the candle had long since gone out.

'It's pretty late and we do have to get going first thing in the morning. We need to sleep.'

Harris still hesitated, shivering. Then, slowly, he got down from the stone ledge. The guns were still roaring. Barton wondered what was happening at the front line. There were rumours all over Feuvry, and their own Battalion repeated them. Nobody knew the truth.

They felt their way back up the steps, hands groping along the walls. It occurred to him that the best thing for Harris would be alcohol – rum issue had been hours ago, he would have to go upstairs for his own flask.

Barton told him to wait inside the front room of the house where most of his platoon lay sleeping, and continued on, in the darkness, up the next two flights of stairs. He was more than half-way there, because he felt his foot come up against the broken section and made a note to take care, when the shell came and the blast of it threw him backwards down the flight. He threw his arms up over his head to shut out the appalling noise.

At the foot of his report to Brigade Headquarters on the incident of the night of September 19/20, Col. G. T. C. Garrett commanding 2nd Battalion at Feuvry, gave it as his opinion that the town was unsuitable for billeting purposes. The lives of nine of his men had been lost. Those of other regiments to be billeted in the town in future would be unnecessarily at risk. Overnight halts might more safely be made at Beauterre, two miles further south.

122

STANDING ORDER No. 107. Major General Tebbits. Commanding 1st Division. 1.9.1915. The village of BEAUTERRE (Ref. Ordnance Map 48, 4 Miles S.E. of ARTUN) will not be used for the purpose of overnight halts by infantry troops. Billets are to be found in FEUVRY (Ref. Ordnance Map 47).

'David…'

'If I'd left him in the cellar and taken the brandy down to him. If we'd all just left him.'

'If we'd left him he would have stayed there until tomorrow morning, we would have had to fetch Franklin who would have ordered him out, and if he hadn't moved then, he would have been court martialled.'

'He'd have been *alive,* Hilliard, he'd still have been alive.'

'For that matter, if you'd stayed with him yourself for a couple of minutes longer in that room you would have been killed as well. And that is true of hundreds of men everywhere in this war every single day – if, if, if, might, might, might.'

'For Christ's sake you sound like one of our politicians! Have you heard yourself?'

Hilliard came across the room and stood beside him at the boarded-up window. The sky showed through the gaps, grey, as the dawn came up.

He said, 'I'm only telling you the truth because that's how it is out here.'

He had been terrified that Barton had been killed when

he had heard the noise. 'Look, David, I know perfectly well how you feel ...'

'Do you?'

'Yes.'

Barton was silent. In his head he still heard the noise of the shell, he could still feel himself being flung down the stairs. He still saw Harris's face.

'You cannot and you must not spend any more time blaming yourself, saying if only this and if only that, it's useless.'

'Yes.'

'If you go on doing it, you will be useless.'

'Yes.'

But then Barton thought, he is one of them, he thinks the way they think after all, he sees the things they see. He tells me that I know nothing. I have seen nothing, but that is no longer true. Already, he has put Harris out of his mind, the night of September 19/20 is an incident, a report will be made on it, one man has gone from the platoon. That is all.

In fact, seven out of the nine men killed had been from their platoon. The shell had hit the front of the house, coming down into the corner of the room in which they slept and close beside where Harris had been standing, waiting for Barton to come back with the brandy. Four other men had been wounded by shrapnel and falling masonry.

But wasn't Harris better off? For would he not have gone through terror after terror in the front line, only to meet with a death less sudden, more painful, more clearly foreseen? He had been spared all that. He had been alive – and then dead.

Or else he might have lived, to see the end of this war, which everyone in England told them was imminent, would be before Christmas. If, if, if. Might, might, might.

Garrett had asked Hilliard to write to the men's relatives, as soon as they got into the support line the following day. He had been told nothing about the business with Harris in the cellar.

'You could write the letter about Harris,' John Hilliard had said, as they came out and made their way back to the shattered house and the remaining men of the platoon who were clearing up with grey, cynical faces, who had been so abruptly reminded of where they were, that it had all begun again.

'You can write to his parents.'

'Yes, I want to do that.'

'You needn't tell them anything about the fact that he …'

'Oh, for Christ's sake, John, what do you take me for?'

The light was getting paler. They had had no sleep at all. Around them, the shadows of their luggage, boots, rifles. The conversation with Harris repeated itself over and over in Barton's head, there were his own, meaningless, comforting words, used to get the soldier out of the cellar and up the stairs, to his death.

Hilliard was looking at him.

'What's the matter?'

'I don't know. You …' Hilliard wondered how he could tell him. That his face had changed, in the space of a day and a night that his eyes had taken on the common look of shock and misery and exhaustion, that the texture of his flesh was altered, was grained and worn.

'It had to start somewhere, didn't it? But could it have started worse?'

Hilliard said, 'When the shell came I'd heard you on the stairs just before it … I thought you were dead. When the noise stopped, I could hear a man calling out. I thought it was you. I was sure you were dying or dead.'

Barton turned his head and smiled, and then his face changed again, the old, self-deprecating expression over it, and mixed with that, concern for what Hilliard had been feeling. He said, 'I never thought I might have been dead.' Though that was not true.

'No. It's only when you see it happen to someone you've just been talking to, or think about it in the middle of doing an ordinary job in a safe place.'

'Dread.'

'Yes. But you can get another feeling, too – a peculiar sense of detachment immunity. None of this has anything to do with you, only with the others.'

'Harris didn't have that feeling, down in the cellar.'

'No. He was afraid.'

'Does it often happen? Do men often simply break down at the thought of it?'

'No. I've only seen one man in Harris's state before – he was worse than Harris. But it was in the middle of a particularly bad attack and he'd just lost his brother, he'd seen him killed by a mine.'

'I said things to Harris that wouldn't have given hope or comfort to a dog.'

'Yet they did.'

'Did they?'

'They must have done. You persuaded him to come out.'

'Oh yes. I suppose that was some sort of achievement, John.'

'*Stop that!*'

'Why did you come upstairs for me? Why couldn't you have stayed and talked to him yourself?'

'It was pointless, I wasn't getting through to him, I wasn't even getting him to listen. I don't think he so much as realized that I was there. I knew it would be different with you, that you'd succeed where I couldn't.'

'Why?'

'I don't know. Does it matter? I was right, that's the point.'

'I touched him, I held on to him. That's what he needed. That was all he needed. It wasn't what I said to him.'

'You could do it for him,' Hilliard said slowly, 'and I could not. It's what you do for me. You listen and you're there. That's all. It's the same thing.'

Barton lifted his head. The skin beneath his eyes was chalk white and crossed finely, like tissue paper. He looked exhausted. 'You're still alive. That's the difference,' he said. 'Harris isn't.'

Hilliard wanted to put his hand out and touch him. And could not.

Coulter came up the stairs to wake them.

And so we came on here and now we are in support trenches behind the front line. After what happened last night I don't believe that I can ever be badly shaken again. I have, for instance, been quite unmoved by the sight of unburied bodies lying about here, just as they lay about in Feuvry. They are all along the sides of the road, and out in the fields, in shell craters, and piled up on top of the trenches like sandbags. Some of the ones in the craters are Germans. Doesn't the enemy have the right to a decent burial either? But why ask that, since so few people have any sort of burial at all during the offensive – scarcely during the whole war, it seems. No time, no time. And yet some of the men say there is all the time in the world, the days drag along. But I have been ashamed of myself for getting so thoroughly hardened so quickly. John says I am not, that this is just a sort of numbness after shock, everyone gets it at first. I wonder. Perhaps I do not know myself at all. I was so appalled at the broken buildings and so little worried by the broken bodies. That cannot be good.

I have been reading Sir Thomas Browne, who comforts me, because I learn great truths, which I have read and passed over before, simply because I had nothing to relate them to, in my own experience. 'Christians have handsomely glossed over the deformity of death by careful considerations of the body, and the civil rites which take off brutal terminations.'

Well, that is not true here.

I have never in my life been so tired as I am today, and the difference seems to be that it is not a healthy tiredness. John feels it too. We both look at one another's faces and remark and change and know. We don't bother to say anything about it. The rest camp, the orchards and the quiet lane and the path alongside the stream, all have receded far away, they seem like some dream country which we inhabited long ago: though I cannot truly believe that we were *ever* there, and that we were so contented and had no quarrels with anyone, and that the sun shone so kindly.

Though it has been shining here again today, there seems to be no sign of any move into real autumn weather. The men are glad of that, they tell me about the horrors of rain which brings the mud, and I listen and believe them, so I'm glad that it is dry, even though this means water rationing. And everything smells so much worse, too, under the sun.

Since we got here we have done nothing but work. Until this evening, at least. And now I have to write that letter to Harris's parents. They live in Devon. I am putting it off. John is sitting opposite me making his way slowly through the other letters about the dead men. Captain Franklin came in to see how we were getting on – I could see (and feel) John bristle the moment he came through the curtain. He really is not so bad, though, just a cold fish. John's face gives nothing away except his own tiredness. But how angry it makes me that we should be sitting here doing this at all, because the whole accident was so pointless, the men were doing nothing except sleeping and waiting for today. I am glad there has been so little trouble for you with bombing, after the early scares, because shells are frightening, and they make the most shocking *noise*. But I suppose one would rather be catapulted out of sleep into death than to have to sit and watch it creeping up on one. Though one or two of those men did not, in fact, die at once, they were half blown to bits but lasted various lengths of time, waiting for the ambulances to come. I'm sorry to pile on these agonies but I need to tell you. I shall only keep back what might worry you unduly. But then, in your heart of hearts you will know, all of you, and we have never kept even unpleasant truths from one another.

We have a reasonably comfortable dugout in this trench. John says it is more than 'reasonably comfort- able' which shows only how much I have yet to find out! You come along the trench, which is quite narrow and zig-zags crazily, so that you lose your way after a yard or so, in all the right angles – and the dugout is cut into the bank. We have a corrugated tin roof, and sacking in front of the door. Someone kindly labelled it, years ago, with 'Chez Nous' written on a broken bit of wood, and nailed up. It remains. Inside, it's sur- prisingly spacious, we can both stand up and stretch our arms out without *quite* touching! There are two bunks (hard) and a table of sorts. And all the paraphernalia we brought with us, of course. You've no idea how much one has to carry with one in the army. Not to mention all the clothes one wears and the bits and pieces strapped about one's person. Still, one thing we do have here is a gramophone. There is another at Battalion H.Q. which the C.O. uses to play drawing room ballads, sung by bass baritones. But this was quite unexpected treasure – nobody knows who originally owned it, but now it goes with the other fixtures and fittings. I suppose someone brought it down and then was killed and it was never returned or auctioned off. There is a small and very curious selection of records. I wonder if you could manage to send some of mine out? Only a few, and I shall have to think about exactly what, because they'll be heavy and I don't want us to be even more loaded. I'd like to take the gram. into the front line trench but John laughs a hollow laugh and points out that we'd never manage to hear a thing. Also that it does belong here. I take the last point, but one of our Lewis guns sends cheery salvoes over every few minutes and I have proved that there is only one point, as they actually fire, at which you simply cannot hear the music at all!

Now – I seem to have written myself out of the awful depression I felt when I sat down. Reading the last paragraph, I sound almost cheerful. Well, and Coulter has just come in and he is always enough to make anyone perk up. We're still sharing him, especially after the losses of yesterday. One of those men was to have been my batman here. I wonder when we shall get replacements. John says one of the hardest things is having to get used to new faces, new faces. Some you never get to know at all, they don't manage to impress themselves on you. Nobody could say that of Coulter though. But he isn't 'a card'. The platoon does have one of those, a man called Fyson, who is not bad if he's kept under, but he becomes rather tedious, especially as his stories and jokes are both fearfully obscene and very un-funny – unpardonable combination!

As I have worked myself into this better frame of mind, I must write to the parents of Private Harris and get it over. And I really do want to write. Only it will be such a *deceit*. I have learned a great deal about deceit, since coming to this war.

Then it will be the beginning of my first night in a trench. There won't be much to do. We were to have begun with carrying parties to bring up all the stuff we need to mend our wire and get the trench cleared up and the sides strengthened, but because of last night's loss of sleep, all that has been put off until tomorrow. It makes me wonder how long we are all intended to be here. Rebuilding trenches will be rather like repairing a house – presumably people are going to be staying in it. I should have thought the object was to get out as quickly as possible and move into the enemy trenches ahead. It doesn't look as though anyone expects us to move for the rest of our lives. But really there is no telling what is supposed to be going on.

I hope we manage to get some sleep. I seem to have gone beyond tiredness, into a kind of daze. I need to sleep.

Glazier is doing tonight's duty because he was in a different billet last night and they missed the direct shelling.

But it was after all, an easy beginning. For two weeks, they stayed mainly in the support trenches, and fell into some sort of routine, they were getting used to things, it was quiet enough: there was time to play the gramophone.

'Boring,' Barton said once.

Hilliard raised his eyes from the pile of ration returns. 'I'd rather that. So would you if you've got any sense.'

'Come on, John! Where's your yearning for excitement? The sound of battle "where ignorant armies clash by night". Doesn't that stir your blood?'

'No. And that isn't especially funny either ...'

'You know, you haven't much sense of humour, have you?'

Hilliard considered for a moment. A man went past the flap of the dugout, whistling. No, he thought, no, I have not, and David has, it is one of the things I most envy in him. Once, he himself had simply been called 'a bloody prig'. He had a glimpse of himself down all the years of the past, stiff and reserved, anxious to please – but humourless. Barton burst out laughing. 'All right, all right – don't look so stricken!'

Hilliard smiled, went back to the ration returns. And felt, as he was writing, a sudden, warm pleasure, a sensation of being comfortable here, at home and in comparative peace, doing dull, easy jobs in Barton's company. He was happy. Barton was still reading Sir Thomas Browne.

For some time longer it went on like that, and the weather, too. September passed and there was still sunshine, hot in the middle of the day and with the smell of autumn on the damp, misty mornings. The men were in good spirits.

'Cushy trenches,' Hilliard overheard one of them say – Hemp, the pastry-cook from Brighton. Hilliard repeated the phrase to Coulter as he stood outside the dugout one morning shaving from a tin mug of lukewarm water, looking at himself in the mirror he had propped up against a sandbag. The sky was a thin, flat blue and high overhead a lark hovered and trembled, singing.

'Cushy trenches!'

Coulter looked troubled.

'Well – aren't they?'

'Maybe, sir.'

'I think they've passed us over, forgotten us.'

'They're getting it badly up at Chimpers, sir.' Chimpers – the village of Chimpres, not more than five miles away. Hilliard remembered it from the early days of June. There had been very little left of it even then.

'Again?'

'So I hear, sir.'

'You do manage to hear a lot, Coulter!'

For once, his batman did not return the smile.

'What's up?'

'I don't know, sir. Just a feeling.'

Hilliard glanced at him and was alarmed. It was not like Coulter, who was a cheerful man and usually grew more cheerful, at least on the surface, the more immediate the danger. But he himself had come to respect these forebodings, to know what they might mean, and it was not only Coulter who had them. All through the spring and summer he had come across men who were experiencing 'just a feeling' – that today it had their number on it, they would not come through. He remembered Armstrong urgently telling him about a letter which he carried in his breast pocket. If he was killed he wanted Hilliard to be sure and take the envelope and send it home as soon as he could, it had 'something special' in it. Armstrong had been in France since the beginning, had gone, with Garrett's Battalion, through the early battles, Ypres, Loos, and then the whole of the Somme, and had remained quite unscathed. He led a charmed life, the others said, bombs fell within inches of Armstrong and missed. Once he had stuck his head recklessly over the parapet and been rewarded with a sniper's bullet, which had whistled through his hair and stuck in the earth of the trench behind him. He had volunteered for night raid after night raid, three times he had been one of only a handful of men who had returned safely. He survived and a superstition had grown up around him. If you stuck with Armstrong you would be all right. But on the morning they were waiting for a barrage that began their attack on Belle-Maison, he had been beside himself with trying to impress upon Hilliard the urgency of the letter which he carried. He had 'had a feeling'. Hilliard had taken little notice though he had promised to take and send home the letter if the time came. Armstrong went over the top with the first wave and was hit almost at once, Hilliard had seen him crumple after no more than thirty yards.

But Armstrong had not been the only one. And there were other men who felt quite differently, who had suddenly known confidence that they would be all right this time. It was as though they were surrounded by an invisible steel cage, impenetrable by shell or bullet, so that they pushed ahead through a surge of fire and knew, were sure, that they would be safe, if only because they were marked out for death at some later date.

Once, Hilliard had been led over the open ground and then along a treacherous sunken road to the 8th Division trenched in the middle of a heavy raid, and the runner who led him had known exactly where and when to leap and duck, run or stay still, he had said afterwards, 'I knew it was all right today. I had a feeling.'

That had been Baxter, who was still alive, Baxter, with the four front teeth missing and hair shaved as close as a convict's. Hughin's brother-in-law. A year ago, Hilliard would have scoffed at such forebodings and superstitions, 'the feelings' of the men. In the line. Not now. Now, Coulter was saying little, his face was worried. 'Well, it's quiet enough here for the moment. Don't start putting the wind up everyone.'

The man looked hurt and reproachful. He knew more than the officers about the importance of morale.

'Have you finished with the water, sir?' He spoke politely, and the distance opened between them for a moment. Hilliard wanted to make amends, and could not think how.

He went inside. 'Coulter's got the wind up.' The dugout was dark and stuffy after the bright sunlight of the trench. Barton was getting ready to go down the line and take a foot inspection – though, because the weather was dry and the spirits of the men were so good here, they looked after their feet well, obeyed regulations to the letter, changed their socks and oiled themselves as regulations dictated, they had the time and inclination, there were no problems with infection. Barton was tightening the laces on his own boots.

'What makes him think that? Has anything happened?'

'No.'

'Perhaps it's just too quiet for him all of a sudden. You know how he's always longing to have a go!'

'Maybe.'

'Why is he bothered today, especially?'

Hilliard shrugged. 'He's got a feeling.'

To his surprise, Barton, who did not share his knowledge about the way the men thought, did not know the truth which so often lay behind their forebodings, looked worried himself. He sat on the edge of his bunk for a moment, entirely still.

'I should think Coulter knows what he's about,' he said,

'doesn't he? He keeps his ear to the ground, he always seems to know what's going on, long before we do.'

'Yes.'

'I should think he's worth taking notice of.'

'There's nothing we can do.'

'We can listen to him.'

'We haven't heard anything.'

'But it *is* too quiet.'

'Yes. I feel jittery myself, now and then.'

Barton looked concerned.

'No, it's all right. And this does happen, you know, and it can go on for weeks and months. Especially if they're concentrating on another bit of the line. We could perfectly well have a whole spell like this, mending the trenches, mending the wire, messing about with report forms and rifle inspection and nothing else at all.'

'And you think we will?'

'How should I know?'

Barton looked at him carefully. In the end, Hilliard moved quickly towards the table, the pile of letters waiting for censoring. 'No,' he said, 'on the whole I agree with Coulter.'

Barton got up and went out and he looked cheerful then, looked almost relieved. John Hilliard realized that he knew so little about him, there were so many thoughts and feelings he could not share, reactions he was unable to predict. Was Barton tired of this suspended existence? Just as the men had become irritable and restless in the camp at Percelle. Did he want 'excitement' as he had teased Hilliard earlier, want something, anything, to happen? And if so, why? For he had no feelings about the justness of this war, no anger against the enemy, no desire to fight and kill for the sport of it and no reason for personal vengeance, unless you could count the death of Private Harris.

Hilliard did not know. But this was superficial, nevertheless, for the ease they felt in one another's company was so great now. Hilliard had never shared so much of himself before, never been so simply content. There were times when he caught Barton's glance, or walked behind him down the trench, when they sat in their dugout in the evening, reading or doing paperwork, listening to the gramophone, when Barton laughed suddenly, teasing him – at those times, he felt a welling up of pride and pleasure and love. Then, he wanted to say something, though he never did.

The letters from Barton's family included him always and automatically now, there were long paragraphs from these people he knew and yet had never seen, addressed entirely to him, and he read and re-read them and could not believe that he had been so easily accepted, was part of that charmed circle, of Barton's life and family, of his past and present. It was as though he had been standing in a dark street looking into a lighted room and been invited in. He had ceased to feel any alarm at the arrival of the letters, with their messages and questions for him, he ceased to want to draw back from their intimacy. So that, when he received a letter all of his own from Barton's mother and then, almost immediately afterwards, from

one of the married sisters, he had flushed with amazement and pleasure, had brought out the sheets of thin
white paper again and again, to read when Barton was not
there, unable to believe in them, unable to take in the fact
that he meant something to them, that they had written to
him. He stared at his own name on the envelopes:

My dear John.
Dear John Hilliard.

They had begun so. And at the end of Barton's own
letters, the messages:

Love to your friend, John.
Remember us all to John H.
We do hope you are both of you well and in good spirits.
Do let us know if John gets any leave, and he can come
and see us, even if he is not with you.
Thank John for his messages.
You are to share the things in the parcel with John, of
course.

He said again and again, 'They don't know me. They
don't know me,' holding the envelopes, looking at the
writing upon them, feeling the smoothness of the letter
paper between his fingers.
    As always, Barton laughed, 'Of course they do!'
    'They haven't seen me, we have never met.'
    'Oh, that's practically superfluous by now.'

'They …'

'What?'

But he could not say. He only lay awake, and heard Barton turning over in his bunk and listened to his breathing, and thought about these people, thought, let it go on, *let it go on*. He did not mind Barton's teasing now, had even come to want it, did not mind anything he said or did. It was enough that he was here with him. In the night he woke and heard the guns and his heart thudded, he sat up and said aloud, *'Jesus,* God, don't let him be killed, don't let him be killed.' And did not even mind, at that moment, that Barton might have woken and heard him. 'Don't let him be killed.' Barton had not woken.

12 October 1916.

I don't know quite when I'll get the time to write again. We are said to be moving up to the front line within the next day or so, though we have no official news. Things are apparently rather bad up there but so far we have had very little direct shelling in these trenches and only two casualties. I think we shall be spending most of our time on fatigue parties, and especially at night, as there is a terrific lot to be done. John says all this is bound to mean Business, but we can't say more than that – and in any case, know nothing for sure. But they have been in battle over to the east of us. I should think it must soon be our turn.

You ask me if the memory of things I have seen stays with me and if I am continually upset. Yes, I suppose so – that is the answer. Yes. There are two things which I shall not be able to forget, I think. One, the death of Harris. But the other may seem to you more trivial. As we were coming up here from the town in which we spent that awful night, the men were in quite a cheerful mood, in spite of what had happened, I suppose because they had had some sleep and the sun was shining. They were singing and marching rather gaily and in place of Harris's harmonica someone had got a pipe – we were like soldiers in those poems about the Jacobites! The road was very busy and we passed a good many men coming from the front. But once, just as our song was particularly rousing, we came face to face with a Regiment who had come from some of the worst fighting since July. They were obviously a very depleted lot: their uniforms looked as if they had been on their backs for a year, they were dirty and exhausted, marching raggedly and in total silence. When they saw and heard our men, going so cheerfully up the road, their faces were shocked and grey and they stared at us – Oh, it was like meeting ghosts, their looks were so knowing and so accusing, they were so old and worn and sad. And as they were so silent so our men, too, faltered and the song died away and we went on very soberly. The grins and laughter in our Battalion turned sour, I looked at one or two of my own platoon and saw that they were remembering – it was like being caught roistering at a funeral. We were ashamed of ourselves. And I know I shall not forget that – those men, the expressions on their faces, everything about that moment. At the next halt our men were very quiet, smoking and lying about on the edges of the grass, suddenly face to face with it all again.

And yet – why shouldn't they sing while they can? One asks oneself that too.

What else is there to tell you? It is still good weather, we are still sick of the food, but your parcels keep us going, and John gets some quite amazing things in his expensive Fortnum's hampers. We had jars of preserved ginger and figs and chocolate liqueurs and goodness knows what else. It's rather sad that his family can spend so much money on parcels and so little time in writing to him – and such short letters. It's easy enough to order a hamper for someone else to pack up and despatch. But it has nothing to do with me, and who am I to talk, since I so much enjoy what comes in the hampers! He likes to hear from you, though, I do know that, so perhaps if you can find the time you could go on writing to him occasionally? He doesn't say much about it, but I know him well enough to be able to tell from the slightest sign whether he is pleased or depressed or whatever. We are really quite happy here, it has been the greatest good luck, our meeting and coming together. It has meant my missing all of you has not been quite so bad – I do, of course, terribly, but somehow, having John about has taken the edge off it. I am sure you will all be glad of that, too. And I think I may have been good for him. He is a different person, even in so short a time – more relaxed, if nothing else. He doesn't seem to be so afraid of himself. Perhaps that sounds strange?

I must write to Nancy today. I was very pleased about the prospect of her new infant. Tell her I cannot possibly have another godchild, four is quite sufficient for anyone, but she is welcome to call it after me if it is a boy! I told John about it. He looked surprised that I should know, so early on. I gather his family don't talk about these things – he ought to have been a doctor's son!

Tell Amy the socks are fine. I don't need them yet but when the weather gets colder, as it is surely bound to do before very long, I shall be pretty glad of them. The men tell horrifying stories of almost freezing to death, once autumn and winter set in, of having to break the ice on the water and toes freezing and dropping off, and heaven knows what else.

I am not really afraid of going right up into the front line permanently now, since my whole war so far seems to have been a succession of stages, I am being gradually broken in. And there have been respites in between. I suppose this is one. It is just so dull and boring and, at the same time, so tiring. One longs for a bed! (The bunks do not qualify for that grand name.) Thank you for the records, which came beautifully packed and quite undamaged. We have been playing the Elgar and the Schubert – especially the latter, most of all. The 'Winter Songs' somehow don't clash with this golden autumn weather at all, they contrast, and besides, they are so beautiful to hear, after the unharmonious crashing of shells and guns in the distance. Not to mention the singing of our own men and Coulter's whistling and the clatter of dixies and bayonets. Oh, it is not quiet here, not really! Only it is rather better towards the end of the day.

The Adjutant came in yesterday and listened to the whole of the Frühlingstraum' (it is John's favourite) and then just walked out again, so we could not tell if he approved, or enjoyed it, or was puzzled, or what! He is a strange character but most efficient and the morale and general state of the Company is very high. I have to give him a good deal of credit for that, though John would hate me for saying so, since his dislike of the man has not waned. And I agree that he does view the pair of us very coldly. But one does not know what his circumstances are, he may be a very unhappy man. He is a lone wolf, certainly, and maybe he thinks we should all follow suit. But then, John has always been a lone wolf, I think, until now. Perhaps out of necessity rather than choice, however.

Someone has come in with a message for me. Do send more apples if you can, they are marvellous.

'David…'
'All right. I'm ready.'
'I wish you weren't going.'
'Why?'

'I mean – I wish I were going instead.'

'Do you? Whatever for?'

Hilliard stammered, 'It's only that you …'

'What?' Barton looked up, grinning. It was late in the morning. Warm again. Barton was to go up into the front line, led by Grosse, and along to an Observation Post from which there was a good view of the ridge and Barmelle Wood, and the few ruined walls to the west of that, which were all that now remained of Queronne. The whole site was held by the enemy. He was to make a map and bring back as much information as he could about the area.

'Why you?' Hilliard asked now.

'I'm better at drawing.'

Hilliard felt his heart swollen with fear. He thought, he does not know what it could be like, he doesn't *know*. It was, apparently, a straightforward job, no more dangerous than anything in the front line now. But how dangerous was that? It had been clear and quiet and still here all day. When the order came down and Barton had gone to see Franklin, Hilliard had sat at the table in the dugout and trembled with fear. He would rather go himself, he would rather anything. As usual, Barton had laughed at him, and he had seemed excited, too, proud to be given this job. When he was getting himself ready there had been a gleam in his eyes of something like real pleasure.

Hilliard thought, he won't come back. Anything can happen between here and there, one small thing is enough. The front line had been under heavy fire all week.

He won't come back.

Perhaps this was the feeling that Coulter and the other men got when they were sure, when they knew. And they had generally been right, hadn't they? Perhaps this was it.

He wanted to go to Franklin and demand to be sent on the job himself, though he knew he could not, and that it was all insane, for sooner or later Barton had to come up against a real danger, the risk was constantly there of his being hit, wounded, mutilated, blown to bits. Or simply shocked, as he had never been shocked before, by some appalling sight or sound.

But Hilliard had never known this kind of fear, not even on his own behalf during the summer, and certainly this agony of feeling on behalf of someone else was entirely new to him, he could not cope with it all. All that morning he had scarcely been able to look at Barton, and yet when he had looked, had not wanted to take his eyes away. For he was there, now, across the tiny, dark space of the dugout, everything of him was there, his skin and flesh and bone, whole and unblemished, he was there, calm and confident and cheerful, his manner as always easy, amused. Hilliard could still reach out a hand and touch him if he chose. He was there. Later, he would not be there.

He shook his head, and in a second of absolute clarity, he saw that nothing mattered except Barton and what he felt for him: that he loved him, as he had loved no other person in his life. The reason for this and the consequences of it were irrelevant, the war was irrelevant, something for them to get through. Nothing else could be truly important again. Nothing else.

Acknowledging this for the first time, he felt as though his head had been rinsed through with clear water, and he was no longer perturbed, he had seen and accepted it all. Everything else was far away. He looked down at the pile of ammunition returns on the table in front of him, at the black lead pencil and the box of matches. At his own hand. And then the fear hit him again, broke over him like nausea. If Barton were killed what would he do? What would he do?

'Mr Barton?'

'Yes. Hello, Grosse. I'm ready when you are.'

'Right, sir.'

Grosse was from Glazier's platoon, one of the best runners in the Battalion, though he was large and clumsy looking, with huge hands and feet and an enormous, wide head. He stood in the doorway. Coulter came up behind him.

'The C.O. would like to see you, Mr Hilliard, as soon as you can.'

Hilliard stood up at once, grateful for the interruption, for now he would not have to watch Barton go, hear his footsteps retreating behind those of Grosse along the trench, would not have to sit here and stare at his papers for hours on end, waiting. They both went out of the dugout together without speaking again, turned their backs and went in opposite directions.

Battalion Headquarters was in a half-derelict cottage standing on its own at a crossroad half a mile from the support trench. Behind it, in a field which had once been ploughed and then overrun by the army, so that it had deep ruts, dried and caked in the sun, there was a trampled path, the grass was brown-yellow. In one corner, the rusty remains of a plough.

Looking behind him across the countryside Hilliard saw no signs of life except the white dust from the guns in one direction and in the other from the trucks coming up the road. The lines of sandbags forming the trench parapets were pale brown and grey in the sun. The landscape was flat and featureless here, apart from a few trees, which had been split and stunted by shells through the previous summer. The guns fired from the enemy lines and then their own replied, and in the lull that followed, blackbirds sang and sang.

He wondered why Garrett had sent for him, whether it was a routine matter or whether Coulter had been right, and 'something was up'. But nobody else had been summoned, so far as he could tell.

'They wanted a plan of the whole section of country just there. I thought young Barton would do it. I thought he'd make the best job of it. He's got a good eye, hasn't he? Yes, I should think he's got a decent eye. It'll be experience for him.'

The C.O. pushed a box of small cigars across the table towards Hilliard. He looked ill again, the effects of the boost given to his morale by the move out of rest camp had vanished. His skin was a bad colour, yellowish grey, so that Hilliard wondered if he might not, in fact, be physically ill. But the bottle of whisky was on the desk beside him.

'I wanted to have a word with you, Hilliard. I thought it would be as well to put you in the picture – in so far as I have a picture, that is.'

Hilliard wondered why. When something big was coming up there were full briefing conferences. But Garrett had always singled him out, had liked to confide in him, tell him things, even trivial, irrelevant things, had asked him for his opinion, he seemed to place some kind of confidence in him. Now, he shuffled some maps on his desk, stared at them, took up a pencil and began to circle it in the air above one of them as he talked. 'You'll hear all about the details when they come in, but I'll tell you what all this is about. You're going up into the front line in a couple of days. Not sure exactly when. I suppose you've heard what's going on up there?'

Hilliard did not reply. And he did not want to hear, not today.

Barton had been gone almost an hour now.

'Oh, I know the rumours that get about, and rumour doesn't always lie, not out here. Well, it's merry hell at the moment, though it's rather worse ten miles or so further east. I don't know exactly why – we haven't been doing much. The Boche seem to have got the wind up. But what we can expect pretty soon is the date of an attack they're planning for the 2nd to make on Barmelle Wood. They want to have another go at it. The Hampshire tried to take it in July and the City of Londoners last month – perhaps you know? They lost a hell of a lot of men. The trouble with that place is it's on a ridge, and they've got perfect cover, they can simply look down and take their time until they see us coming up, and it's just bloody good target practice for them – that's all. The Hampshires lost most of their men before they'd gone a hundred yards. You can't advance up a slope like that, no matter how good your barrage is, and get away with it.'

But this had been the pattern of the whole summer here, Hilliard thought, this was how the Big Push had come, and failed, this was what it was all about.

Garrett did not pause or glance up at him, but gradually his voice had taken on an edge of sarcasm and of disbelief in the ignorance of those who were planning this new offensive in precisely the same way as the old, those who were so many miles away. His contempt for the men who looked at maps and moved pins about upon them was scarcely veiled at all. Hilliard was still surprised, even knowing the C.O. as well as he did, surprised that he should allow himself to talk like this before a lieutenant. But 1 July had changed him, he no longer cared greatly about anything, except for the men under him.

'Well, you know what all this will mean. Preparations once you get into the line, all day and all night, fatigue parties, wire parties, reconnaissance raids.'

Hilliard's heart sank.

'Yes.' Garrett lit another of the cigars. 'I know what you're thinking.' He paused, then, in a burst of real anger, said, 'Those bloody raids are a waste of time, arms and men, and I have said so until I am sick and others have said so and we might as well save our breath, save our breath. You know all about it.'

Hilliard did.

'Well – there it is. There's more of it to come. I don't suppose it's much of a surprise to you? No. Meanwhile, of course, they want to know everything about the German line here, everything about Queronne and the Wood, everything about everything, and apparently all the information they have got from aeroplanes will not do for them. So our contribution is this little trip of Barton's, out to the o.p. After that, up we go.'

How little did Garrett really care about the war now? Had he told all the others this? Did the Adjutant know? And Glazier and Prebold? No, he had told them nothing, Hilliard was certain of that. Garrett had been to the conference at Divisional H.Q. and heard the plans for this new operation on their section of the line, had been angry and wanted to talk to someone outside his immediate personal staff. He liked Hilliard and trusted him. It made no difference that he was so far junior in age and rank and experience. Hilliard was on his side. Garrett took the risk. He was a democratic man.

'Well, there it is,' he said. 'And the chances are that everyone will have completely new orders this time tomorrow. You know how they chop and change us about. But for the moment, that's the operation.' He paused for a moment. 'Barton will be up there by now.'

Suddenly Hilliard realized that there was more to it than

a simple desire for his company, that Garrett had brought him here to get him away, pass some of the time for him. He saw and understood. Hilliard felt a surge of gratitude.

The Colonel's batman brought tea, with bread and butter on a plate.

'Privilege,' Garrett said wryly. 'You see, Hilliard? This is what rank gets you – sliced bread and butter and tea in a pot. Privilege!' He raised his cup. Then said, 'Young Barton's got a cool head, hasn't he?'

'I – yes, sir. I think so.'

'Reservations?'

'Not exactly. It's only that he hasn't seen any action yet and he's … I wonder how much things will affect him, how much he'll take to heart.'

'He's a sensitive young man, yes.'

'Yes.'

'That's no bad thing.'

'Oh no.'

'I doubt, you see, if emotion will cloud his judgement. He's a valuable sort of man to have around. He keeps us going, but there's more to it. He makes us think twice, Hilliard – helps us not to take it all for granted, to become too cynical. He has some quality we've been lacking – gaiety, composure and sensitivity. He's a good man.'

Hilliard was surprised at Garret's perception and sureness of judgement, surprised that he had seen below the surface of Barton's good humour and charm to what lay below. He felt a keen pleasure, hearing it, wanted the C.O. to go on with his praise and approval. If he could not be with Barton, then he could hear his name spoken, hear the best things said about him.

'Who's taken him up there?'

'Grosse, sir.'

'All right?'

'He's a good runner, yes.'

'I don't want to lose young Barton through some stupid accident.'

Hilliard clenched his hands together under the table. *He won't come back, he won't come back.*

He felt giddy.

'We've had enough silly bloody accidents.'

Garrett drained his tea and looked about for matches. 'You'd better go back,' he said, and now he seemed abstracted, no longer sure why he had sent for Hilliard or what he was going to do next. But as an afterthought, as Hilliard reached the door, he said, 'Keep quiet about all this of course.'

'Certainly, sir.'

'I suppose they'll change their minds, as I've told you, we shall find ourselves shunted off somewhere or other. It may all come to nothing.'

But it will not, Hilliard thought, and knew that Garrett knew it would not. Sooner or later, they would be going up to Barmelle Wood, the ridge, Queronne – they were on the plans, to be attacked and captured now, since they had not been taken that summer. There would be the long, tedious preparations by night, the waiting and the orders and then, over the top. They would take the place of the

Hampshires, who had failed here in July, and the City of London Regiment, who failed last month. For some reason known only to those seated round the tables with their maps, this particular place mattered so much.

So tomorrow, then, or the day after, or at the beginning of next week, sometime, they would leave their dugout with the comfortable bunks and the gramophone, and march a mile along the communication trenches, and up the road to the front line, and into the thick of daily shelling and nightly raids, they would spend hours without sleep, fetching and carrying up and down the dark winding trenches, hours writing more and more reports, and the atmosphere would be more strained and tense than ever. It had been the same in July.

Yet it would not be the same as July, they had been excited then, they had planned for the coming battle, which was to be the last, the battle to end the war, they had been confident and purposeful, jubilant even, they had not minded the tiredness and the heat and the slow, tedious work of preparation, the accidents and the danger.

The first of July had come and gone. And all the days after. It was not the same now. But it had all begun again.

Hilliard dropped down into the trench, and began to walk along towards the dugout. The smoke was going up from the cooking fires ahead. It was quiet for the time being, the guns might not have been there, hidden towards the east.

Coulter came round a traverse. 'There you are, sir. The Adjutant wants to see you. Some trouble over kit inspection.'

'All right. Thanks, Coulter.' He paused. He did not want to go on. He wanted to stay here, in the sun.

Coulter said casually, 'I take it we're not expecting Mr Barton back until dark, sir?'

'No.' Hilliard forced himself to take a breath, to relax. 'No, of course.'

He went to find Franklin.

When they began to make their way along the front line trench, Barton felt excitement churning in the pit of his stomach. It was his first real job, one for which he was entirely responsible, he had nobody, not even John, behind him. Only the runner, Grosse, guiding his way.

He had not been prepared for the full extent of the noise, which was deafening when the shells came over. They were falling very close but they were mainly the heavy sort, which came with a sudden roar and at such speed that escape was impossible. You could do nothing about them, moreover, could not predict in advance where they might land, and so you simply went on, trusting to luck.

The trench was quite deep, cut into the chalk, and at the beginning the sandbags had been renewed and the parapets built up again. But as they went further on, work had ceased, the floor was a mess of rubble, and the sides badly broken. Pit props, shovels and bales of wire cluttered every traverse, and the duckboards, laid in preparation for the coming winter, and the wet weather, were often broken or rotted away.

Grosse went ahead steadily, vanishing every few yards

round a traverse, so that Barton felt that he was following his own shadow, felt time and again that he was completely alone. The chalk of the trench was bright, dazzling his eyes in the mid-day sun. But he was exhilarated, glad that he had been chosen to come here. There was an element of chance, but that did not yet seem to be the same thing as danger.

The shells were whining down often and seemed to be falling in a direct line ahead of them as they walked. Barton came around a traverse and almost bumped into his guide.

'What is it?'

Grosse had his head slightly on one side. 'Just seeing which way they're coming, sir. They're working them to a pattern.'

There was a pause, and then, from nowhere, the loudest explosion Barton had ever heard, his eardrums seemed to crack and his head sang, the whole trench rocked as though from an earthquake. Just ahead, soil was thrown up like lava, and then there was the sound of it splattering down, mingled with pieces of shrapnel, into the trench bottom. As they moved on a few paces, they heard a scream, which came with a curious, high, swooping sound and then dropped abruptly, became a moan. Then, behind them this time, another shell.

Grosse had thrown himself down, his hands over the top of his steel helmet, pushing it almost into his skull, but Barton had only dropped on to his knees. His heart was thudding.

'Grosse?'

The man moved, lifted his head. 'Are you all right, sir?'

'Are you?'

The runner stood up cautiously, brushing down his tunic. His face was still impassive. He nodded.

'Shall we go on then?'

But as they rounded the next corner walking towards the spot from which the cry for stretcher bearers had just gone up, they came upon a total blockage in the trench-way, a mess of burst sandbags and earth, shrapnel and mutilated bodies. Blood had splattered up and over the parapet and was trickling down again, was running to form a pool, mingling with the contents of a dixie which had contained stew. The men had been getting their mid-day meal in this traverse when the bomb had landed in the middle of them.

'Grosse ...'

'Better hold on, sir.'

'Stretcher bearers!'

Barton said, 'Is there an officer here?'

A man was crouching, knees buckled and apparently broken beneath him, and he looked up now, his face white and the eyes huge within it. 'There was, sir.' He vomited, shuddered, wiped his mouth on his tunic sleeve.

Grosse leaned over him.

It was impossible to tell how many men there had been, and now the shells were landing again, following the line of the trench further ahead. Barton wondered if they were going to meet a scene like this at every corner. He found himself staring in fascination at the shattered heap of limbs and helmets, at a bone sticking out somehow through the front of a tunic, at the blood. He felt numb.

The stretcher bearers came up, and sent back at once for more help, to dig the men out and clear up the mess. The trench parapet had a hole blown out of it like a crater.

'We could go on, sir,' Grosse said eventually. His voice was calm.

They went on and for a short way nothing happened, they came across parties of men eating and drinking tea and they made room for them to pass. The shell might not have fallen, such a short distance away, killing perhaps half a dozen soldiers.

They found the G Company Captain and Barton reported his presence to him, he was cleared to continue.

'Get down!'

He got down though he had heard nothing. But the smaller, minenwerfer bombs were different, they could just be spotted, sailing down like crows through the blue sky. They watched, waited, tried to guess where this one was going to fall, ducked again.

Nothing. After a moment, Grosse got to his feet. 'Dud,' he said. From behind, their own guns began to fire towards the German line.

They went on again. He wondered how he was going to sit in the Observation Post and make any sort of accurate map if this heavy shelling went on, and if his eyes were drawn again and again by the sight of the minenwerfers, if he was so tense, trying to gauge each time where they would fall. But he was still somehow unafraid for himself, though his initial excitement had gone long since. Grosse's face was grey with dust and soil. He supposed that his own must be the same.

They turned another corner. A young soldier was up on one of the firesteps, facing them and about to step down into the trench. Barton caught his eye. As he did so, a shot came and the man toppled rather slowly forward, to land almost on top of Barton and between him and Grosse.

Barton stopped. Bent down.

The man lay quite still but as Barton looked at him, a shudder and a quick breath went through his chest, and the limbs jerked and convulsed before going still again, the helmet slipped sideways off his head. His eyes were open and his mouth was full of blood. Otherwise, he seemed quite undamaged, his legs lay relaxed as though in sleep. Barton stared down at him. The skin across his nose had peeled with the sun. He had very pale, almost white eyelashes, and a curious mark, like a smoke burn, across his forehead.

Grosse retraced his steps and was standing on the other side.

'Get a stretcher quickly.'

'He's dead, sir.'

'He was breathing.'

'He was dying.'

'Get a *stretcher*.'

Grosse did not answer. Barton reached out a hand and touched the man's chest.

'Stuck his head too far up, I suppose. Daft thing to do. They're crack shots, they could shoot a bullet through a ring on a pig's nose at a hundred yards, those Jerry snipers.' Grosse leaned against the side of the trench, his voice was conversational.

'For God's sake ...'

Barton looked up angrily. Fell silent. But he did not want to leave the man on the ground. The body was warm, the skin faintly flushed. He had been alive, looking into Barton's face. Then dead. Nothing. Nothing.

A Sergeant came round the traverse. Barton rose to his feet.

'You'd better get a stretcher.'

'Sir.' The Sergeant glanced down. 'Private Price,' he said, shaking his head, perhaps unsurprised.

'Come on, Grosse.'

But he did not want to go on, he wanted to go back, not because he had lost his nerve, but because he was sickened, for where was he going, why was he to spend an afternoon making a map, playing a game, spying and reporting about a few square yards of country, why had the men standing in the traverse with their meal, and this Private with the pale eyelashes, why had they been alive when he came down here less than an hour ago who were dead now? He had wanted to take up the body of the man called Price and dig a grave and bury him himself, for would that not have been more purposeful, would he not have done the first thing of value since coming into this war? Instead, he was going ahead with binoculars and a notebook and pencils, he was detailed to make a map. *To make a map!*

He stopped. For a moment it was quiet. He supposed they must take time off for meals over there, too. Quickly, he pulled himself up by his hands and rested his toes on one of the higher layers of sandbags lining the trench, moved up until his head was at first level with, and then protruding over, the parapet. He thought, I have never done such a dangerous thing in my life. But felt calm. 'Mr Barton …'

He took no notice of the runner. The sun was shining straight into his face, so that when he closed his eyes it was pleasant, it was like sitting outside on the terrace of the house at Eastbourne, basking, soothed as a cat, he felt his skin comforted by the warmth. He half opened his eyes, and the space between the two sets of trenches was pale, in a haze he saw smoke going up, saw grass and a couple of gorse bushes and the shell craters, dried in the sun, saw the enemy wire glittering. There were a few small clouds, very high up in the sky. Nothing moved. He thought, I shall stay here, I shall wait and warm my face in the sun and if they fire, they will fire, if I am killed, I shall be killed. For it seemed not to matter, nobody's life mattered, he was of no more or less importance than the Private who had just spouted blood at his feet.

He was here to make a map.

Jesus Christ!

He felt hands gripping his legs, hauling him roughly down so that he stumbled and lost his balance and landed awkwardly, on the floor of the trench. A splinter of some-thing went through the soft flesh of his palm.

Grosse was standing stiffly, his face furious, and unapol-ogetic. 'I'm sorry, sir, but…'

'All right, all right.'

He got up slowly and made a play of checking that his binoculars had not been damaged. Realized that he must have looked over the parapet and been quite still for several seconds and that no shot had been fired at him.

A heavy shell roared overhead and crumped down quite a way behind the trench. The air smelled of cordite and chalk. Grosse said nothing more. Barton wondered what he was thinking, whether he would tell anyone what had just happened.

'We'd best go on, sir.'

Barton nodded. It was not for a long time that he came to and realized what he had done. But it seemed entirely reasonable, nevertheless, he felt neither ashamed nor surprised. Something had clicked inside his head, he felt different, he would go back to the support trenches and his own dugout, he would talk to John and read Sir Thomas Browne and listen to the 'Winterreise', he would draw his map and make his report, but he would not be the same as when he had set out. Something was new. Something …

He wondered who the dead man had been, remember-ing the sunburn and the open eyes with their pale lashes, the sudden breath. He wanted to kneel down in the trench, then, and press his face into the soil, and weep, out of misery and rage, he wanted never to get up again.

'Thank your mother for the almonds.'

'I'm not writing a letter.' Barton did not look up. His face was closed, whatever he thought or felt was undetectable.

They had moved down here, five miles behind the trenches, and were in tents and some farm buildings in the middle of derelict countryside. Their first tour had been a quiet one, but the men were tired, they had worked long hours at tedious jobs. Within three or four days they would be back and B Company would go into the front line.

'Elgar.'

'I beg your pardon?'

'Or Brahms. We could have the Brahms Serenade.'

'No.'

'What then? Schubert again?'

'I don't really feel like music.'

'Oh.' Hilliard hesitated, fiddling with the head of the gramophone.

It was mid-afternoon. In half an hour he'd have to go and supervise the Company taking baths in an iron tank situated beside some disused stables. Barton went on writing.

'Are you all right?'

'Perfectly, thanks.'

Hilliard wanted to cry out, so helpless had he felt for the past week, in the face of this blankness.

Barton had the green-bound copy of Sir Thomas Browne beside him, he was writing something into a note-book. John wanted to ask what was wrong, to offer help, anything. But since he had come back from his day in the Observation Post at the front line, he had been like this, silent, apathetic, withdrawn, as though he had new secrets. Hilliard felt snubbed. Once he had said, 'What have I done?'

'Nothing, John. Nothing.'

Now, outside, the men were being drilled by Sergeant Dexter.

'David …'

'Yes? What is it?' But he went on writing, his pen moving evenly over the thin paper, he did not look up.

Hilliard realized how used he had grown to Barton's openness, to the warmth of his conversation and his constant teasing, to the long letters and the stories about his family, to his sympathy, the way he gave and shared so much. He had, simply, grown used to receiving from him. Now he was afraid, in the face of this new mood which he could not fathom. David's behaviour had become like his own in the past. 'Moody,' Constance Hilliard would say. 'You were always a moody child, John.' And so the label had stuck and he had grown used to it, almost proud that he preferred his own company to other people's and found silence easier than conversation and gaiety. His behaviour stood for everything which his parents mistrusted, for them his character was flawed. Well then, he had wanted to be flawed. But since his meeting with Barton he had begun to question himself. He had changed. And now?

He rubbed his fingers over and over the black ridges

of the gramophone, needing help. He said irrelevantly, 'Huxtable's got compassionate leave. His father's dying.'

'Oh. I'm sorry.' The writing went on. Barton liked Huxtable, they shared a certain sort of humour. Now, he only sounded polite.

'I'd better go and sort out the bathing facilities. You should come.'

'Should I?'

'Well – it's an entertainment.'

'For whom?'

'Look …'

Barton stopped writing. His expression was perfectly friendly, there might have been nothing wrong at all. But there was something. Something … He did not want to talk. Desperately, Hilliard said, 'I could move. I could have a word with Garrett – I mean, if you need a break. Perhaps that's what it is? We've been together rather. I suppose you might be able to share with Glazier.'

Barton put the cap on his fountain pen and began to screw it around and around. He said, 'I'm sorry. Yes. I'm not very good company.'

'No, it isn't …'

'So, if that's what you want, of course, go ahead.'

'No. I'm thinking about you.'

'What about me?'

Hilliard felt himself sick with the effort of trying to explain what had never before needed explanation, of trying to break through this tension between them, to help Barton or himself. Do something. He spoke very slowly.

'I mean that you have been a bit – quiet. Things are different, aren't they? I thought you probably wanted a break from me.'

'No.'

'Oh. I see. I thought …'

'Oh God Almighty, John, I don't…' But Barton pulled himself up, fell silent again. He was still screwing the cap of the pen between his long fingers.

Hilliard thought, he has got to tell me now, it has got to be cleared up, whatever it is. Now, now. Now he would speak. Now …

The thread of the pen broke. Barton put both parts down on the table, stared at them. The silence went on.

Went on too long to be broken then, there was nothing either of them could say. Dared say. They did not move for minute after minute, standing quite apart from one another in the dark little tent.

In the end, Hilliard walked quickly across to the flap, ducked, went outside.

The sun had not been out all that morning and now heavy-bellied clouds were piled up overhead. It would rain.

The men went up, singing, to the communal bath and made the most of it, twenty at a time in the grey, scummy water, but cheerful, splashing and floundering and waving to the war photographer who had been with the Battalion since the previous day. The air smelled of carbolic and chlorine and of the rain to come. Hilliard stood, pitying them their lack of privacy, the way they

were always herded together, and yet envying them too, their carefully ordered life and clear, uninhibited friendships and enmities.

And then he checked himself, for it was more dangerous to think like that, why should this life at war be any more simple, any less full of conflict for the men than for Barton and himself, for Garrett, for any of them? He knew nothing about the men, why should he patronize them? And he thought, too, that none of them knew or greatly liked him, as they liked David. He felt miserable, entirely alone. He wanted to go back to the front.

Let them not complain about immaturity that die about thirty; they fall but like the whole world, whose solid and well-composed substance must expect the duration and period of its constitution.

It is a brave act of valour to condemn death but where life is more terrible, it is then the truest valour to live.

We term sleep a death and yet it is waking that kills us and destroys those spirits that are the house of life.

Themistocles, therefore, that slew his soldier father in sleep, was a merciful executioner: 'tis a punishment the mildness of which no law hath invented.

After a battle with the Persians, the Roman corpses decayed in a few days, while the Persian bodies remained dry and uncorrupted. Bodies in the same ground do not uniformly dissolve, no bones equally moulder.

Men are too early old and before the date of age.

Adversity stretcheth out our days, misery makes Alc-
mena's nights, and time hath no wings to it.

But man is a noble animal splendid in ashes and
pompous in the grave, solemnizing nativities and
deaths with equal lustre, nor omitting ceremonies of
bravery in the infancy of his nature. Life is a pure flame
and we live by an invisible fire within us.

'Tis all one to lie in St Innocent's churchyard as in
the sands of Egypt. Ready to be anything in the ecstasie
of being forever, and as content with six foot of earth as
the glorious sepulchre of Adrianus.

'Which of these is right? Which do you really believe?' For
having read them, Hilliard wanted to understand, he was
moved by what was written.

'Why are you reading those?' Barton was standing in
the entrance to their tent.

'I wanted to see what you'd been writing.'

'Why?'

'I thought it might help.'

'Help what?'

'I – I suppose I wanted to know what you were thinking.'
'And do you?'

Hilliard looked down again helplessly at the sheets of
paper, the neat, black script. There was silence again. He
read, 'Men are too early old and before the date of age.'

Barton crossed to his side of the tent, and opened his
valise. 'The C.O. wants to see us. Everyone.'

'Oh. I suppose we're going back then.'

'Probably.'

'It's a relief.'

'Is it?'

'Well – I don't much like it here. I never liked this sort of halfway house. One foot in the war and one foot out of it. The men aren't very cheerful.'

Barton shrugged. 'What difference does it make, John? Does it matter where we are?'

The camp was dreary, badly equipped. It had begun to rain late that afternoon, a thin drizzle, while the men were still bathing. The estaminet in the nearby village was grubby, the faces of the proprietor and his wife sour and unwelcoming. And a mild dysentery had broken out among B Company.

'I hate it here,' Hilliard said. He had been tense, the last few days.

'Yes. We'd better go and see Garrett.'

Barton had walked across to the packing case that served them as a table, put his hand on the papers which Hilliard had been reading, as though to cover them up or take them away. Then he seemed to change his mind, lose interest. He left them as they were.

Hilliard said, 'I like reading them. I like the pieces you've taken down.'

'Good.'

'They seem to set it all at a remove, don't they? And he gives a shape to something shapeless, gives it all a point, somehow.'

'Does he? What point has it?'

'I thought – well, isn't that why you read him? To try and make some sense out of all this?'

'The war? I shouldn't think that's possible.'

'Perhaps not.'

'You've never really thought it was, have you?'

'No. So you don't read this because it helps things?'

'I don't know what I do or why, John.' Barton sounded weary.

'Why did you take these particular sections out and write them down in a book by themselves? They must mean something.'

'I really don't know. It was something to do.'

'Oh come, that doesn't sound like you. That isn't the kind of thing you say.'

'All right. Perhaps it puts a neat fence around things – tidies them up. I just do not know.'

Hilliard felt again that he had come up against a hard wall, he did not know what to say or how to go further. So often in the time since they had first met he had half-phrased some thought, groped his way towards the precise expression of what he was feeling, and David had at once understood, had picked up his meaning and stated it for him, or expanded it. Not now. Now he blocked everything in the same dull, tired, patient way. He had lost his gaiety and also some edge of understanding. Or was trying to lose them, to numb himself. Now, he asked, 'Are you ready?'

'Yes.' But Hilliard still lingered beside the papers. He said, 'I wish I could make a pattern out of things like this. Sergeant Hurd keeps a diary. Did you know?'

'Yes.'

'Perhaps that's what he does – makes a pattern. I wish I could make one. Make sense of it.'

Barton shook his head. 'So do I.' He turned to go out of the tent.

It was raining heavily. They walked slightly apart, John Hilliard a pace behind, so that he saw Barton's shoulders and the side of his head but not his face, not his expression. He felt again the appalling sense of his own failure, a misery that he could say nothing, do nothing, that he did not know.

Glazier joined them and walked beside Barton, began to talk about hunting. He was a well-meaning man and rather lazy. Once, David had suggested that he might also be callous, but when Hilliard had pressed him, asked if it were because of the foxhunting, he had shaken his head, said, 'No. Anyhow, perhaps I'm wrong, perhaps it wasn't a fair thing to say. I don't know the man really. It's just – I wonder if he cares much.'

Yet now he seemed to come alive for Glazier, more than at any time during the past week, he talked with something of his old, teasing manner, laughed, so that Hilliard, a pace behind, felt jealousy rising in him, he began to hate Glazier. But hated David, too, for giving so much of himself away so freely to another: he thought, what has Glazier got, what does he say or do, that I cannot? What spring has he managed to touch?

They separated going into the briefing conference in the dingy cottage which was Battalion Headquarters. Barton sat across the table from both Glazier and himself, hands together, listening and silent. When he caught Hilliard's glance, he returned it calmly, and then, the second time, smiled, a vague, dispassionate smile. Garrett told them they were moving the following day.

He woke to a sound which he could not at once identify: it was not only the rain which had already churned up the field outside and soaked under the tent flaps, so that their ground-sheets were wet and muddied. There was the soft rumble of water on the canvas. But something else, a tearing noise. He realized that the lamp was on very low, and shaded by a valise which had been propped up on the packing case in front of it.

'Barton?'

'Damn. I'm sorry – I hoped I wouldn't wake you up.'

'What's happened?'

'Nothing and I've nearly finished. Go back to sleep.'

Hilliard stretched. His limbs were cramped and he was damp and chilled. There was the close, mouldy smell of wet grass and soil. The tearing noise had stopped. Barton was sitting down, only the top of his head was visible over the upright valise.

'What are you doing?'

For a moment he did not answer. Then he said, 'I suppose I found out that whatever I'd been trying to achieve didn't work and shouldn't work. I mean that I *ought not to have tried at all.*'

He spoke very quietly but there was a note of despair in his voice.

'I couldn't sleep and I knew why. I'll feel better now. Look, I didn't mean to wake you.'

Hilliard was standing. 'It's not particularly comfortable anyway.'

'No.'

'I'm fairly wet. That would have woken me up before long. I don't seem to be able to be wet though I get through most other disturbances. I slept for six hours in a trench at Ancerre, with half a hundredweight of earth and a dead man on top of me.'

Barton did not comment.

'You can get used to almost anything, you know.'

'But should you?'

'Well, it helps to be able to sleep. You have to sleep when you can.'

'I don't mean things like that – sleeping, getting used to the food, the rats and fleas and noise. I mean ... other things.'

'I know.'

'I thought about you just now. I've been sitting here for a long time thinking about you. You've had more time to get used to things, haven't you?'

'Some things. Yes.'

'And yet when you went back to England you couldn't sleep, you had nightmares, you couldn't even bear the smell of the roses. It all came back then, the men you'd seen die, the noises and the smells. You hadn't forgotten.'

He seemed to be asking for some kind of reassurance, that this was truly so, that Hilliard had remembered, and suffered for it.

174

'You know I hadn't. I told you – I've told you more than anyone.'

'Yes.'

'David, what *have* you been doing tonight?'

He moved across the tent and looked over the valise at the packing case-table. His green-bound copy of Sir Thomas Browne, and the notebook into which Barton had earlier copied the quotations, lay in a pile, torn into small pieces, the leaves ripped from the binding. There were only a few pages still left intact, he had almost finished when Hilliard woke.

'You can't make a pattern out of it, you cannot read a book and get comfort from fine words, and great thoughts, and you shouldn't bloody well try.'

'I don't know …'

'I do. I've got to face it, it is wicked and pitiless, it is all one Godawful mess, and how can I sit here and let that man, that great man, lull me into a kind of acquiescence? Be romantic about it? Is that right? Is that how he would want to be used?'

'You were reading the Psalms, too.'

'Yes. Or the Psalms or anything. You asked me if it all "helped". Well, if it did it should not have done so.'

Hilliard sat down on the canvas stool beside him. He said, 'Hasn't your father used anaesthetic? And why do we give the men rum issue?'

'For God's sake …'

'Isn't it the same?'

'No.'

'I wonder.'

'No, John. It's one thing to numb yourself against some kind of pain, to get up courage for an ordeal. This is different, this is a question of basic attitude. I've been trying to set everything apart, make it grandiose, give it a point and a purpose when there are none.'

'Perhaps the men wouldn't agree with you – not all of them. Coulter thinks there's still a reason for it all, for him it is a just war, he'll go on till he drops.'

'I'm not Coulter.'

'You're not being fair to yourself, all the same.'

But it is all right, Hilliard thought, now it is all right again, at least we are talking, he will let me get through to him. He felt enormous relief and a kind of gratitude.

'I told you about what it was like in the summer and when I went home afterwards. I think that was a good thing, for me anyway, because you made me talk and it was what I needed. I couldn't talk to anyone else.'

'No.'

'I haven't forgotten any of what happened in July, I haven't accepted any of it. But I still feel better for having told you.'

Barton smiled and his face lost its withdrawn, formal expression. 'Oh, you should have been a family doctor, you should be a C.O. or a priest! Except that perhaps you would be too conscientious, and I can see through you like a mirror. You are thinking, "What a good thing it will be if only I could get David to spill it all out, how much better he would feel!" Oh, I'm sorry, John, you've been trying very hard with me.'

'Yes.'

'But I have never felt like this in my life before. You must see that. I haven't known myself. I didn't know what to do.'

'I've felt it. I know.'

'Yes. Perhaps we're alike then?'

Hilliard hesitated. 'No,' he said eventually. 'We're not. And it's a good thing. It's just that we happen to have had the same responses to a situation.'

'It was going up into the o.p. that day. I saw eleven men killed. I suppose that doesn't seem many to you. It was to me, when there wasn't even anything in particular going on, it was a "routine day". Eleven men. There might have been more only that I didn't see them. And there were all those bodies lying out in the shell craters and they'd been there for weeks, months – I don't know. They were all swollen and black and the flies were all over them. And I had to sit there and draw a *map*. I saw ...' He stopped.

'What? Tell me.'

'No. No, you don't need me to go on.'

'But it would be best if you did.'

'Haven't you had enough of it all yourself?'

'That isn't the point,' Hilliard said gently, and knew then that he had learned all this from David, learned how to listen and to prompt, and why, even learned a tone of voice. Not long ago he would not have been able to do it. He wondered if there was anything that he had not learned from David.

'But the worst of it has been that I haven't known how

to face myself. That Private who was snipered – looking at him I could have wept and wept, he seemed to be all the men who had ever been killed, John. I remember everything about him, his face, his hair, his hands, I can remember how pale his eyelashes were and I thought of how alive he'd been, how much there had been going on inside him – blood pumping round, muscles working, brain saying do this, do that, his eyes looking at me. I thought of it all, how he'd been born and had a family, I thought of everything that had gone into making him – and it wasn't that I was afraid and putting myself in his place down there on the ground. I just wanted him alive again, it seemed the only important thing. I just wanted to stay there and look at him, I couldn't take it in, that he'd been so alive, and then he just lay, spouting out blood and that was that, he was dead, nothing. Or something. I don't know. But dead as far as I could see, his flesh was dead, he'd had all that possibility of life and it was gone. Like Harris. A bloody silly accident. If I hadn't been with Grosse I'd have stayed there, I think I would have lain down and never got up again. I wanted to bury myself. Do something. Only – God, I had to make a map, I had a job to do, so I went and did it and I suppose that took my mind off it. By the time I'd been there an hour and by the time I came back into our dugout, I'd begun to accept it all. I was used to it. A man was dead – eleven men were dead. So? It was happening every day, it was no different because I'd been there. It would go on happening and there was not a thing I could do to stop it. In fact, my being here was helping it continue. I felt nothing then, just nothing any longer. I didn't think I could be unfeeling, but I was. Callous. Counting the bodies in No Man's Land and trying to see if they were ours or theirs, guessing how long they'd been dead as a question of academic interest. I had watched stretcher parties scrape and shovel up what was left of half a dozen men, along with what was left of their meal and the side of the trench. I heard a Sergeant tell them to go for more help, to get more tools and put down some duckboards, they weren't making a good enough job of it. They did. They simply did it. And ever since I've heard the shells going over, and thought, that's so many dead, so many wounded, one or two dozen, that's next door, that's the right flank trench, where did that one go, and Oh, Pearce is dead then, I'm sorry to hear that, yes, I'll write to his wife, give me his papers, I'll do the form. Last week, the day I went to the village to see the *Q.M.S.* – that day it hit me, that I'd been feeling nothing, I'd become entirely callous, I was taking it in and not letting myself think or feel anything. I was reading Sir Thomas Browne in order to abstract it. I'd never been so ashamed. You said that you can get used to things.

'I knew that. But although you were cool on the surface that is only because you are made like that – it *is* only the surface. You'd told me all about the summer, and how you felt when you went home, about what struck you most when other people there talked about the war and how it had to go on and I knew you hadn't forgotten, you didn't stop feeling any of it for a moment. But what was happening to me? What *has* happened to me?'

He had been tearing and tearing at the paper, the pieces were tiny like confetti in a pile before him. Now, he brushed his arm across them so that they scattered, dropping off the packing case and lying, white as flowers, in the mud.

Hilliard said, 'But you haven't forgotten either. You haven't stopped feeling. You have just told me as much.'

'That boy…'

'You can't feel every man's death completely and all of the time, David, you simply cannot.'

'Every man's death diminishes me.'

'Yes. So you have just told me the truth, haven't you?'

'Have I?'

'That you *are* diminished and know as much. And you are changed. And ashamed. That you feel it. Some people would scarcely have noticed how many men were killed, they've gone past it, it's all become part of the day's work.'

'That was how I felt.'

'No, you didn't, not really. Shock does strange things, you should know that. Some men do not even suffer shock.'

'What kind of men are those?'

'Precisely. But all the same, you know as well as I do that if you are here and doing this job, you have to shove things out of the way all the time. We'd never carry on at all otherwise.'

'Then I wonder if we ought to "carry on at all"?'

'If you truly believe that, you can go and say so to Garrett tomorrow, register as a conscientious objector – lay down your arms. I imagine it would be hard – it was hard enough for your brother, and he hadn't gone through the business of joining up and serving. But if that is what you feel, then you must do it.'

Barton looked up. 'It would be funk, wouldn't it? I went through all that before I came out here. It would be funk.'

'You hadn't seen anything then.'

'All the more reason why it would be funk and seen to be so.'

'Are you afraid of what else is to come?'

'I'm afraid of myself. Of what I am becoming, of what it will do to me.'

'Are you afraid of your own dying?'

Barton's face lightened at once. 'Oh, no. I've thought about that too. No. I have never really been afraid of that.'

'It is a brave act of valour to condemn death, but where life is more terrible, it is the truest valour to live.'

Barton smiled. 'I've just torn all that up.'

'But I have just learned it by heart.'

'And is it true?'

Hilliard considered. But he found himself thinking instead, whatever was wrong between us is wrong no longer, and will never be so again. He was certain of that.

He said, 'It isn't going to get any better. It is not going to stop being more terrible. None of that nonsense about its all being over and done with by Christmas, about our driving them out like foxes from cover. I scarcely believe that it will ever be over. At any rate there is no point in thinking so.'

'But I asked you if it were true that where life is more terrible it is the truest valour to live.'

'Isn't it something you have to make up your own mind about?'

'Is it true for you, then?'

'Yes,' Hilliard said. 'It's true. I think so. And you?'

'I don't know.'

Barton was looking down at the scattered shreds of paper. 'What a philosophical night!'

'No. We have been talking about what is happening, about yesterday and today and tomorrow.'

'Yes. Do you suppose I ought to gather up the remains of Sir Thomas Browne?'

'He's stuck in the mud.'

'A sort of burial. Fitting.'

'Yes. Though as a matter of fact I'm rather sorry. I wanted to borrow the book and read it for myself.'

Barton stood up and put his arm across Hilliard's shoulders, his face suffused with amusement. 'Don't worry, I've got another copy at home. I'll get my mother to send it out to us!'

'Do that.'

A gust of wind blew the tent flap open, blew rain inside.

'It's going to be bloody wet and bloody cold,' Hilliard said looking down at his groundsheet. They ought to finish their sleep, though he had no idea of the time.

Barton let his arm drop, and moved a pace away. He said, 'I love you, John.'

Hilliard looked at him. *'Yes.'* He was amazed at himself. That it was so easy.

'Yes.'

PART THREE

Yes, I know you will have been thinking that something has happened. I'm sorry. But there were various troubles which I won't go into now, because they're resolved or under control anyway and more practically, I simply haven't had a chance to write until now, we have been shifted about so much, nobody has had the faintest idea what's been going on. We had a shocking march up here, we have scarcely unpacked for a week and your letters are only just being sent on to me, after long delays – which shows that nobody else knows where we are, either! I suppose there may be others of yours still to come. The upshot of it all is that, we have come further north and that it has rained solidly for a fortnight. We are now in the front line trenches and under heavy fire the whole time. No farther than 150 yards away from the enemy. Why we moved from the last place is a mystery – we had thought they were fattening us up for the kill there, but apparently not and in any case all of our movements seem to be a mystery, we go when and where we are told. Perhaps someone knows why.

The rain. Yes, they all told me what it would be like, but I wasn't really prepared for it and nor was John, because of course he didn't come out till last spring, by which time the worst of it had cleared. The trenches here are very bad, under about 2–3 feet of water all the time. Of course we have trench pumps and of course they don't work so the men spend much of their time baling us out with great ladles. Pretty useless and the rain just fills us up again. We live all the time in waders and mackintoshes. But I doubt if I shall ever feel truly dry again. I cannot believe that only a couple of weeks ago the ground was cracked and parched with the sun, and we were still passing through the last of the fruit orchards.

We have a tiny dugout which has been shelled a few times in the immediate past and patched up badly. It smells, it's under a bank and the roof is only broken timber reinforced with some sandbags. There are two bunks of wire netting, which is useless. The old dugout in the supports was like a Grand Hotel suite in comparison and we have lost the gramophone – I mean, we were forced to leave it behind. I feel it may be a good thing. We have been in very low spirits and physically exhausted, very depressed altogether – our heads feel black and blue (if you see what I mean) from constant noise and alarums. It would have been hard to listen to Schubert and Elgar and be soothed, only to be dragged back so roughly into this present every other minute.

Besides, we have simply had no time.

John has had an appalling cold and sore throat, I suppose because of the wet feet and wet beds – wet generally. We have lice for the first time – a pleasant addition. And rats, which are what I *really* cannot cope with. You will remember how I used to secrete white and other mice in the house – well, don't worry. I shall never be able to look any sort of verminous creature in the face again. And what faces these rats have! Really evil, and they are so bloated and fat and fit looking, they are scurrying about the whole time, you never know when one will come up. They feed on the corpses, of course, of which there are plenty and our own new ones are added every day. There was a battle here about a month ago, leaving the place in a terrible state.

Everybody is on digging parties during the day, rebuilding and sandbagging, down at support line and then back here at night. There is no rest at the moment, and we snatch what sleep we can – we don't seem likely to be relieved.

At night the parties have somewhat got to carry on

as usual through the mud and rain, struggling to bring up the supplies, food and mail and all the stuff we need for our digging and repair work and so on. It's much worse in this weather, it takes so much more time – with water up to your thighs and shells bursting all over the place, you often feel like simply giving up and lying face down in the water. The duckboards are quite useless. But somehow it is still tedious and fairly point-less work: imagine trying to patch up derelict houses in the middle of nowhere all through a pouring wet autumn night! We are drones not fighting men. Not that I want to be a fighting man. But John says that at least there's a feeling of doing something positive, having one clear objective, in a battle. I suppose that means the men are 'dying for the cause' whereas here they are simply shelled or snipered at random in the middle of dinner or foot inspection or sleep, it is like a road accident on an ordinary day, you feel resentful because of the sheer waste of it all.

But I am feeling very resentful altogether now – I have seen enough. The men sing 'I want to go home' and they mean that they want to see their families and that they are sick of all this tiredness and wet and cold and din. That's what I mean, too, but more, I want to be out of it all because I feel guilty that I'm here, and doing nothing to stop it – even if that were to mean bringing it to an end in some great, violent push. And I also just want to be comfortable again and sleep in a bed and have dry socks, to wander about where and when I choose, and to see you all – oh, but you cannot imagine how we long for the small everyday things, scarcely worth mentioning, scarcely noticed at home.

I think we have been brought up here because of some attack planned on the enemy trenches but really we do not know, it might simply be because we're good at repairing. We thought we were going into battle at the last place, before we went down to reserve camp, but nothing came of that. It's all hearsay.

You have never seen such a desolate place as this, it has got uglier and uglier the further up we have come and now it doesn't look like a land made by either God or man, it was thrown up by some prehistoric monsters or devils with no sense of anything but chaos. The road coming was just like a river, with trucks and cars and horses bogged down in the mud and what houses were left just a few bits of wall sticking up out of the ground. As far as the eye can see it is flat and wasted. There are some stumps of trees left and at night they take on all kinds of weird shapes, lit by the Verey flares. The men tell one another they have seen spectres and dead Germans rising up, and although nobody believes it there is a fashion for telling these rather crude ghost and horror stories just now. It's amazing how many people can produce a tale of haunting when called upon.

The ground is full of craters and of course *they* are full of water. A canal not far from here overflowed its banks. I suppose that didn't help the general water

level, and bodies which had been lying at the bottom
since July all came to the surface and were spewed over
the countryside.

Ahead I can just see the enemy line and their sandbags, poor devils, they are in just the same mess as
we are, suffering all the same problems, I can't blame
them for strafing us all the time just to relieve their
feelings. Their wire looks horrifying. It's much deeper
and thicker and more carefully set up than ours, even
though we spend all night and use bale after bale of
the wretched stuff, which cuts into your hands even if
you have gauntlets on. Of course, their shells just keep
breaking it all down.

Well there, I have told you what it's like and made it
sound bad because that is the truth and I would have
you believe it all, and tell it to anyone who asks you
with a gleam in their eye how the war is going on. A
mess. That's all. I shouldn't say that but we censor our
own letters, unless we're unlucky enough to have one
stopped at random going through the next sorting-post.
I'll chance it. Tell all this to anyone who starts talking
about honour and glory. I know you will understand,
though John, who has been reading this, says he could
not write such things to his own family. They believe
we are making advances the whole time, that by Christmas we shall all come home as conquering heroes, that
every death of ours is really a nail in the coffin of the
Boche, and we will chase them out of France like a pack
of dogs, over the top of the hill. He doesn't complain

to them about his physical condition, either, as I have been doing to you. But in fact he has far less resistance than me – hence his cold, which I have not had and nor did I get the dysentery which went the rounds not so long ago. My only injury so far has been some kind of small sore on my foot where I must have trodden on something. Scarcely worth going all the way to the M.O. to complain about!

I almost gave up a short while ago. I can tell you about it now. A deserter is shot if found, of course. I had come to feel that I would rather be shot. You will be ashamed of me. But in fact I did not intend to desert, I had thought of surrendering as a conchy. I didn't and will not do so now. I can't say any more about it here. I would need to sit round with you all and talk about it. I am better, in any case, I think I have come out of the other side of whatever wood it was.

But I am no longer so gay and light-hearted. I keep worrying that when you see me you will notice changes. But a few days with you at home would restore everything. The men, in spite of their weariness, keep us all sane, particularly Coulter and the Platoon Sergeant called Locke. He is a fisherman from Suffolk, and tells us amazing stories of storms and lifeboats and also of long days spent fishing miles off shore, when the water is smooth and glitters like silk and the wind drops and the fish pour into his nets and he rocks in his boat and smokes a pipe and is the happiest of men. Oh, I envy him: he will go back to it and ask nothing more. He has five sons. You wouldn't think he'd be at home here but he is more good-humoured and long-suffering and patient than anyone, and behaves as though most of the younger men were extra children of his! He is also very religious though in a rather stern way. He talks to the young privates when their swearing gets too blasphemous or obscene, and it is as though he is really hurt by it. He gives us all good advice about marrying nice wives and rearing broods of boys! We love him, because he is so straight and conscientious.

Everybody grumbles about the wet and the food and the general low state of health, everyone is on edge with being shifted from pillar to post but there is still this constant, grim good humour, jokes fly back and forth, nobody is cantankerous. Otherwise we would all have given up long ago. Every now and again Coulter gives us his pep talk, about how we are going to 'go out there and show 'em'. I think he isn't entirely convinced that John and I share his fighting spirit, but he never gives up!

LATER

We have had a very bad day. Trench flooded and like a river again. But the shelling has been simply awful. We were strafed for about three hours without a break and all we could do was to sit tight and watch and pray. The C.O. and the Adjutant had just come down and they spent part of the raid in our dugout. We all huddled together in the near dark and every minute or two there was a crash and we all avoided one another's glance. Earth kept thudding down on the roof – I thought we were all going to be buried alive. When I did have to go out into the trench I felt a lot safer. Then there was a constant cry for stretcher bearers. The C.O. went up and down several times in the middle of it all. The men like and respect him for it. He looks very ill though. He brought a bottle of whisky with him and left it for us to finish when he went. Neither of us much likes whisky but we have been needing it, I can tell you.

Captain Franklin is imperturbable, as cool as a cucumber. Very efficient, which the men also respect. They know he isn't going to lose his head. John says he may have a head to lose but certainly not a heart. I wonder.

For much of the time when we emerged into the trench, we could see nothing beyond about 20 yards, for the smoke and mud being sent up in great spouts like water from a whale. The noise was unbelievable. It's like being in a tunnel with trains both roaring towards you and coming at you from behind, and then going on over your head, screeching and wailing. And then the crash crash, crump crump. I thought my brain, or at the very least, my eardrums, would burst from the din. A lot of men had been sent fancy ear-muffs and plugs and heaven knows what other bits and pieces by well-meaning aunts at home but you would need a lot more than some rubber or cotton wadding to shut out any of this. I should think you must be able to hear it all where you are. Every gun of every size must have been trained on us for the whole of three hours. We lost a lot of men. The Suffolk Sergeant whom I told you about just above, which upset us all, and a subaltern called Glazier, who was horribly mangled but lived for a while, in a terrible state. He was, I'm told, incredibly brave and kept on telling them not to bother to send down stretcher bearers, he wouldn't live to need them, they were to save them for someone else. I had never liked him much, and so had occasionally gone out of my way to be friendly to him – a bit hypocritical, but I'm glad I did now. I'm sorry he's dead, because he was looking forward to leave which was due shortly, and which would come nicely at the start of the fox hunting season. He lived for hunting. They did fetch a stretcher party for him which was, as it happened, the worst luck of all, because no sooner had they got him on and gone a few yards than they were all hit, which meant three dead men instead of one and we needed all the stretchers and bearers we could get.

John and I are quite unharmed.

The worst thing apart from the noise and mess is being so *thirsty,* after the constant breathing in of shell dust and cordite and so on. Your throat feels as if it's being burned out. Well, and after all that, nothing came. We had, of course, been expecting an attack, the Germans were surely on their way down into our trenches, the men had fixed bayonets the whole time, and were waiting and waiting – Coulter, I may add, with something near to glee. He can't wait to get his bayonet stuck into someone, which I find very chilling, and more so because he is basically such a nice chap. But when the strafing finally stopped, everything just went quiet. They left us to pick up the pieces. I don't know what the point of it all was. Garrett said they were expecting us to retreat out of here, but we couldn't have done so successfully, and in any case, nobody thought of it.

Now we are left in the mud and rain to begin the dreary business of repairing the damage as best we may and getting the dead moved. B Company has lost 2 officers and 3 wounded, and about 30 of other ranks. Very bad indeed for one day's shelling.

I hope you got the note asking for the Sir Thomas Browne. It's on my fourth shelf, a blue book. I'd also like the Japanese verse anthology and *The Tempest,* if you can send them, and a good novel, which choice I leave to you – just in case I ever get five minutes for reading. The same address, though it is all taking ages, as I told you. No, I have no news of leave and shouldn't hope for any yet. I have no idea about Christmas. It's all the luck of the draw.

John sends his love. He is much better at getting through all this than I am, in spite of his not being well. He's kept me going lately, though he would say that the boot's on the other foot. But that cannot be true, I've not been fit company for anyone lately. Even

Coulter remarked that 'Mr Barton looks a bit seedy', which is his way of saying 'bad tempered'. Have you a chance of getting anywhere to buy me a few postcards with reproductions of paintings on them? I'd like Turner, particularly. Don't go to a lot of trouble or expense. But I should so much like to look at something as far as possible removed from this dun, grey, muddy scenery. I think of you all having been in Wales with great envy. I should like more than anything else to be at St David's now. Or anywhere. But I'm here because I'm here because I'm here!

'How do you feel?'
'Wet. I'm sick of this.'
'Yes. What's it like down at that end?'
Barton sat on the bunk and began to unwind his puttee. 'Much the same. Race got his legs blown off this morning – that shell we thought had landed behind out of the way, I think. Apparently, it didn't.'
'I can't remember which one *is* Race?'
'Glazier's platoon. The one with the odd eyes.'
'Odd?'
'One blue, one green.'
Hilliard was still amazed at how much Barton took in, how many of the men he had come to know well, the small things he remembered about them. He said, 'If you stay here long enough you'll be a C.O.'
'I wouldn't want to. Promotion isn't my line.'
'You'd make a good C.O.'

'No, because I'd tell them the truth; I should have a demoralizing effect.'

'That is exactly the opposite of what you do. You keep us all going, you should know that by now.'

'There's something wrong with this sore on my foot. It looks a peculiar colour.'

'Let's look – did you cut it?'

'I suppose I must have.'

'You'd better get dressed. Go and see Farquharson.'

'Not with this. Anyway, I want to eat and sleep. I'll stick a dressing on it myself if it doesn't heal up.'

'My father sent us a bottle of brandy in the parcel today. I've only just got around to opening it. And some quince jam.'

'Praise be!'

Hilliard found a cup and poured out a good measure of the brandy and handed it to Barton. Then he said, 'There was a letter from my sister.'

'Beth.'

'Yes. She's getting married. She says on Saturday. I don't know which Saturday – that could be tomorrow, I suppose. Tomorrow is Saturday, isn't it?'

'Yes.' Barton put a finger into the alcohol and was dabbing it experimentally on to his foot. 'Anaesthetic,' he said.

Hilliard touched the envelope which lay on top of the opened parcel. 'You can read it.'

'Do you want me to?'

'Yes.'

Barton took the single sheet of thick paper.

Dear John,

It is so nice to have your letters and we are glad to know you are fit and cheerful. We wish you were home but it seems that things are going well from what we read in the papers, and that you will all be back before very long. This letter will come to you with a parcel from father, but it is really to let you know that I am getting married on Saturday. It will be quiet, though there will be what mother calls 'a few' (and I think are a lot!) people back here for luncheon afterwards. We shall miss you, of course. It may seem that it has all been arranged suddenly but I have been thinking about it for some time as I told you when you were home and we have been planning things here for a while. There has seemed no time to write to you.

We are going to the Isle of Purbeck for ten days and after that I shall be Mrs Henry Partington, The Lodge, Astor Avenue, Hawton.

Do write. I must stop now, there are so many things to do you wouldn't believe. I shall never be ready. Mother has a marvellous new lilac dress and coat in silk from Worth, for the wedding.

Our love to you and all kind wishes from Henry.

Beth.

Barton held the letter for a long time after he had finished reading what it contained, for he did not know how to comment, it was so brisk and cool and distant, so lacking in emotion or character. John had talked about his sister, but mostly as she had been when they were children. What was she like now, what did she conceal beneath this formal letter in the plain, dull handwriting? He thought of the long, loving, detailed letters from his own family, which came by every mail and the difference between them. He wished suddenly that John had no father or mother or sister, so that he would be able to bring him entirely under the wing of his own. These aloof strangers ought not to exist at all.

'She said she was going to marry Henry Partington.'

'Yes. You told me.'

'He's a lawyer. He is a dull, stuffed, crass, insensible fool and he will put my sister in a rich home like a padded cell and she will give luncheon parties and tea parties and dinner parties and knit socks for the men and believe that we shall all be home by Christmas and be dutiful to the son by his first marriage and in a short time she will become indistinguishable from my mother – except that she will never be so beautiful or so elegant. She will be quite content and whatever she used to be will have gone, be buried. I'm glad I'm here, David, because I would truly rather be in the middle of this than sitting in that church in a tight collar and then sitting at our dining table and hearing my father make a dull speech and Henry Partington make a stupid speech, and the vicar and Beth's godfather and … I should go off my head.'

'I'm sorry.' Barton reached out a hand. 'I'm sorry.'

'Oh, that's enough of it. I'm sick of the whole business.'

'Yes.'

'But poor Beth! And how happy she sounds!'

'Does she? Is that a happy letter?'

'Did it seem a miserable one?'

'It seemed – I didn't get the impression that she *felt* anything at all. It's so – formal.'

'She is, now.'

'What you should be doing is drinking some of this excellent brandy.'

'How's the foot?'

'Hurts. Go on – have some.'

'Yes. Then I've got to do these letters – oh, I'm sick of reading other men's secrets, I feel like Paul Pry every day.'

'I wish Coulter'd bring up the dixie, I'm hungry and I'm dropping asleep on my feet and I daresay I shan't get more than a couple of hours anyway.' Hilliard had slept while he was out in the trench, supervising the carrying party.

'Talk of the devil.'

'Speak of angels is what you should say, sir!' Coulter ducked involuntarily as a shell roared overhead and crashed somewhere far off, down the road. But it had been quiet tonight and all the previous day. 'Message from Captain Franklin, sir.'

Barton looked up. Hilliard read the slip of paper, got to his feet. 'No sleep, no supper – get your boots back on, Second Lieutenant Barton.'

'Oh Lord ...'

'A nice little reconnaissance party all the way out there through the lovely mud, in a downpour, just the sort of adventure you'd have enjoyed at the age of nine. Coulter, send Sergeant Davies up here, would you please?'

Barton was pulling his boots on again, and then the rubber waders, reaching to his thighs. He caught Hilliard's eye. 'It's what you've been promising me,' he said, 'a recce party? I've been looking forward to it for weeks.'

'Quite.'

Coulter ducked his head back inside briefly. 'Cheer up, sir. It's stopped raining and they've been nice and quiet as mice across there for hours. Just right!'

'Coulter …'

He went again rapidly, his boots making a slopping noise down the trench. Hilliard paused a moment. Then said, 'It's absolutely bloody pointless. Even if the rain has stopped. We won't be able to see a thing, it'll be like going through mud soup, we'll get soaked – what the hell do they think they're doing? We can see all we want to see of their lines from the o.p. during the day and they've been sending planes over every half hour.'

'What are we supposed to be finding out?'

'Oh, everything.' Hilliard began to look about for his compass and stick. 'All possible information you know. Everything.'

'Time spent in reconnaissance is seldom wasted,' Barton said. 'Field Service Regulations Part I Chapter 6.'

Hilliard shot him a look.

'Will you go and meet Davies? We need eight volunteers,

but don't let Devine come, though he'll ask to – he isn't fit. And not Lawrence, either, he'll make a noise enough to wake the dead and then panic. Tell them to black their buttons and their faces. And you do the same of course.'

'What with?'

Hilliard smiled. 'Mud, dear boy, mud. If you look carefully you should find the odd bit of it around somewhere. All right?'

Barton was watching him with something like glee. He said, 'Who was talking just now about potential Commanding Officers? What about you? You're enjoying this, it's exactly what you like, getting something organized, giving out the orders, making sure it all goes like clockwork. You should be a General before you're forty.'

'It helps to pass the time, that's all.'

'Oh, come! You *enjoy* it.'

Hilliard stopped in the doorway, looked back. 'No,' he said. 'No, I don't. And nor will you.'

'Well, you can cope, anyway.'

'That's not exactly the same thing, is it? Are you ready now?'

Jenner and Moreton had been cutting the wire but there was still a good deal to get through before they made enough of a gap for the party to go out. Hilliard sent Coulter back to the dugout for his own pair of wire cutters, bought in the Army and Navy Stores. Waiting, he had a sudden recollection of that day, it seemed like a dream, a mirage of heat and sunlight and elegant crowds, of idleness and chatter and money to be spent at heaped counters, he could not believe in it. The wire cutters were far more use than the standard issue, with which the two men had been struggling.

There were six of them, besides Barton and himself, and including Coulter. He looked at them and saw how ludicrous they were, smeared with mud, their steel helmets exchanged for the ugly, dark woollen balaclavas.

The air smelled moist and thick with mud and stale shell dust, but there was still a faint sweetness, as in any countryside after rain. The sky was completely clouded over – the dry spell would not last. Along their own line they heard the night sounds, the breathing of the men coming up the trench with nightly rations and pit props, bales of wire, sandbags, the suck-plash of their boots in the mud, and then a bump, a soft curse, muffled at once, the occasional creak as someone trod on a duckboard as though into the bottom of a boat. The evening meal was over, and because of the rain it was hard to light fires now, even in the deepest dugout, so that the men lived on tins of cold bully beef, bread and jam and the stew which came up in the dixies and was lukewarm by the time it arrived. Only tea was made on the spot and came in the tin mugs, sweet and dark and boiling hot.

The news of their departure was passed along to their own sentries, then they climbed out one by one and slithered between the wire. Hilliard, going last, snagged the back of his tunic and felt his skin taken off.

They got down and moved on their hands and knees, in

total darkness, and at once the wetness of the earth soaked through them. The going was slower than snail's pace. But for several minutes there were no Verey flares sent up. Hilliard, at the far end of the line and a yard ahead, could not believe that their luck would last and as he thought it, a light shot up, green and beautiful as a firework from the enemy line. It soared and burst like a fan, casting a pale, haunting light over the whole area. They had flopped down on to their stomachs at once, heads pressed into the ground. Hilliard felt his face touch against the cold mud. Just behind him, Coulter had gone into a shallow water-filled shell-hole. Hilliard waited. There was a faint splash and plop, like a frog going into a pond, as the batman pulled himself out, half inch by half inch. Eventually, he touched Hilliard's ankle, signalling that they could go on. The Verey flare had died away.

After another few yards, they could crawl on their hands and knees again. But weighed down as they were with revolvers and the grenades and bayonets, they felt the drag of each slow forward movement, their shoulders and thighs were already aching.

At the other end of the line Barton tried to release the cramp in his foot. He could see nothing at all, they might have been down a mine. So where was the point, how would they be able to tell anything at all about the lie of the land or the enemy front line which could not, as Hilliard had said, be seen through the periscopes in daylight, or on photographs taken from their planes in the air?

They seemed to be going on for hours. His foot was throbbing again, and the thought of gangrene flitted through his mind, he smiled at the ludicrousness of it. All the same, he was worried that this was another thing the war had done to him. He usually took it for granted that he was never ill and that if he were it was nothing, he would get better quickly and without complications. Now, a small injury to his foot was worrying him disproportionately, his mind kept returning to it.

Suddenly, they heard voices, he realized that they were much nearer to the German line than he had guessed. The sounds they could hear were the same as their own, the bump of sandbags, shovelling, soft footsteps, the clip-clip of wire cutters. He imagined a similar party, also making a reconnaissance raid, imagined both groups of men crawling steadily towards one another with muddied faces, until they bumped, nose to nose, and panicked, sprawling in confusion and, because they could not see, risked nothing except immediate retreat. It seemed so insane, so like something out of a boy's adventure paper, that he snorted with laughter, and then stuffed his fist into his mouth to silence the noise. He was soaked and cold and cramped, but curiously elated, the whole movement had such an air of unreality. He imagined the report they would put in: 'We progressed through thick mud in total darkness, and therefore were unable to get the expected clear view of the enemy line. We ascertained that there was a line, and that this contained men. This was deduced from the sound of a faint cough, and two whispers. The fact that these were

German men was deduced from the foreign sound of the cough and whispers (see above).'

Again, he almost laughed out loud, and certainly he was grinning, and knew that close beside him Corporal Blaydon had noticed it and was watching him.

They had stopped and were fanning out, wriggling sideways in the mud. Barton peered ahead. Moved a little further. He was very close to their wire now, he heard a whisper quite clearly.

'Nein. Wo ist der Kapitän?'

'Achtung!'

He went still. But they were hammering stakes, he thought, the man had not been calling attention to his presence. Besides, the Germans would not imagine that anyone was mad enough to come out on a raid through this wet and darkness. The hammering noise went on, only slightly muffled and then another, unidentifiable sound, though the voices had ceased. It was impossible to see anything of the trench, even though he moved another yard further forward. The wire was much thicker than their own, and more expertly coiled. All of which they knew. All of which ...

When the shell exploded, it threw Barton on to his back and he lay staring up, baffled, into the darkness, watching the livid flare of the explosion, and then the green of another Verey light. He felt strangely relaxed by the brightness and the patterns in the sky. Machine gun fire, and then another shell, much closer, the Germans must have got the measure of them. Beside him, Blaydon was whispering, 'Get back, we've got to get back!'

Someone was crying out, and Barton wanted to tell him to be quiet before he realized that the man was wounded. He felt himself bump up against something, touched the cloth of a tunic. It had gone dark again and the rifle bullets were coming now, over the short space between them and the enemy front line. There was a soft thud to his left. Then Hilliard's voice behind him.

'Get on with it. Duck and run.'

'There's …'

'Get on!'

Another shell but ahead this time, as though the enemy were trying to block their retreat. As Barton struggled forward, slipped into water, pulled himself out again, he wondered what had happened, what had raised the alarm. He thought they had been entirely unnoticed. Then there was the cry again. He had gone some way beyond it. Someone passed him, he could not tell who, and then, for a moment, he seemed to be quite alone in the darkness. The cry again.

'Come on, Barton.'

'There's a man wounded.'

'I know. It's Coulter. I can't help him. *Get on.*'

'But he …'

'Shut up. If you're down first warn the sentry that it's us.'

'You can't leave him there.'

'He's too bad to bring in now, we'd never find him, we'd never make it. And we shouldn't be talking.'

Gunfire again. Barton was frantic. 'Look …'

Hilliard said, 'I order you to go on.'

Barton felt the water running down his back under the tunic, and mackintosh, and tasted it too, foul and rusty in his mouth. Behind them there was silence now. Hilliard said nothing else. They waited again. Still silence.

Barton got up and began to move forward, crouching and running like a monkey, ready to drop down. Once, a Verey flare went up, but too far away to mark them out, perhaps the Germans had given up, satisfied with what they had achieved.

Then they were back in their own trench, slithering down from the parapet and a long way from the place at which they had come up. There was a pain in Barton's chest from alternately gasping and holding his breath, and from hauling himself forward on his arms.

He said, 'What happened?'

'You went too near, that's what bloody well happened. They saw you.'

'They couldn't have seen me.'

'I was trying to get you to come back, you were practically on top of them. Do you realize ...'

'It's ...'

'Ferris is dead, Moreton is dead, Coulter is probably dead and Blaydon's got a bullet – in his arm, I think.'

A few yards away, some men from Prebold's platoon were filling sandbags. Now one of them came over, handed Hilliard a mug. 'Tea, sir, and there's a splash of rum. It's not very hot I'm afraid. Are you all right, sir?'

'I am, thanks.' Hilliard drank, and then handed the mug to Barton.

'No …'

'Drink it.'

Barton drank. The men went on with their work, perhaps sensing from their voices that something was wrong.

'I've just sent along for a stretcher, sir. The Private who came in just before you, he's got a bullet through his shoulder and his hand's in a mess.'

'Blaydon?'

'I don't know, sir. He's in a bit of a state. We put him in the dugout. Can I get you any more of that tea, sir?'

'No thanks, we've got to get back to the other end of the trench.'

'They got the wind of you good and proper, sir.'

'They did.'

'It was nice and quiet till you went out.'

'Sorry. Everything all right here?'

'Oh yes, they didn't come near us, sir, it wasn't us they were after! We're all right.'

'Good. But you'd better tell the men to watch out for a bit, now they've woken up. Keep it as quiet as you can.'

'We know what we're doing, sir.'

'All right. Thanks for the tea.'

As they moved up the trench they met the stretcher bearers. Standing aside for them, Barton thought he heard a cry again, from out in the darkness.

'Hilliard …'

But he had already gone ahead. Barton waited. Still silence. In the end, he thought he must have imagined it.

Captain Franklin was waiting in their dugout. He said at once, 'You've lost three men.'

'Yes, sir. And one wounded.'

'What on earth happened? They shelled you pretty accurately, didn't they?'

'Yes. I suppose we were quite close. And it was very quiet. They obviously heard something.'

'Then you must have made a row.'

Hilliard's face was stiff. 'I don't think so. We were unlucky. They found out where we were first go and let us have it.'

'What did you see, anyway?'

'Nothing much.'

'Are they bringing up ammunition?'

'I couldn't tell. There was fetching and carrying, certainly.'

'There is always fetching and carrying,' Franklin said coldly.

'Quite.'

For a moment the Adjutant stood, stick under his arm, his face, as always, expressionless. Then he turned. 'Put your report in as soon as you can, will you?' He went out.

'John …'

'Shut up. It's all over and done with. You've never been out there before and it can happen to anyone. It probably wasn't your fault anyway. Now forget it please.'

Hilliard sat down at the packing case, turned up the lamp and began to write. He was still wearing his mackintosh and the mud was drying in his hair.

Barton said, 'Coulter ...'

'Coulter's dead.'

'How do you know?'

'He must be. I saw the state he was in,' Hilliard said shortly. He went on with his report.

It is still raining and very cold. They have moved us back again to where we were before, only in the front not the support line. But things are very slightly better because, in our absence, the 8th Division have been in and made very good work indeed of repairing these trenches. We spent two nights in billets in what had been a convent school which had a rather beautiful chapel with some 15th-century wall paintings. They had been badly neglected and damaged but the men took the place as a good omen for this next tour.

Our dugout this time is only a few yards away from the o.p. in which I sat to draw my map that terrible day – though you could scarcely believe it is the same place now the weather has changed. There has also been some bombarding of the wood along the top of the ridge by our guns, so that the trees there have begun to look a bit like the old familiar stumps of rotten black teeth. It is so easy to destroy landscape, it takes a couple of days of really bad fighting and strafing, plus this rain, to turn what was beautiful (in spite of the war and everything littered about) into the most frightful scarred waste. I feel we shall have this on our consciences every bit as much as the deaths of men. What right have we to do such damage to the earth? After all, you may say that man can do what he likes with himself but he should not involve the innocent natural world. John disagrees, he says that a tree grows again and grass covers the craters in no time, but a man is dead, is dead, is dead. The animal and bird life seem to survive as a sort of undercurrent to the life of the war, but I wonder how much we have destroyed of that too, and what it is like for these creatures to live down in the earth among the bodies, and to be deprived of leaves and grass and thickets for cover, or to live in the air which is rent by shell blasts and full of dust and smoke and flying metal objects. The men are forbidden to keep pets or to feed the birds, but some of Prebold's platoon had a hedgehog to which they were giving bits of meat and sweetened tea. It then began to dig itself into the side of the trench among some of the sandbags, to hibernate. Until Fakely from that platoon (a strange and rather vicious person) began to get nervous and told everyone that hedgehogs were unlucky and boded evil and death (as if anything didn't bode that, out here!). But he got himself believed – superstition, like the ghost stories, is rife here just now, it seems to pander to the prevailing atmosphere of fear and the constant tension, and also to add a sort of spice to boredom. So in the end they dug, and dragged the wretched small hedgehog out of its dark hole and slung it over the parapet, where it lay on its back, half stunned, half dormant. I happened to be going along just then and saw the whole incident. I can truthfully say it was the first sign of any kind of unfeelingness I have encountered here. I was very angry, irrationally so, and sickened. I then did a most stupid thing, which was to climb up over the parapet and go through the wire and crawl on my belly to retrieve the creature. I might very easily have been shot – I was a good target. Whether they thought I was attending to someone wounded (they often hold their fire if that happens, as we do) or whether I was simply not seen at all, I don't know, but miraculously, there was complete silence, the enemy might just as well not have existed and I got back safely, the hedgehog in my hands. It was crawling with fleas and most prickly. I felt a very great fool but I put it back in the hole in the trench side and covered it up and if it doesn't get blown out of hibernation into kingdom come it may live to see the spring and perhaps even a quieter world.

The men simply thought I'd gone off my head, though perhaps they also wondered if I wanted a way of Putting An End To It All! I felt ashamed of myself. And I have been thinking ever since that I felt incensed and hurt on its behalf and yet I had not thought of going out again and trying to bring back Coulter, after we'd left him in No Man's Land that night. I have been haunted in my sleep and in my waking by the sound of his voice crying out, I have not been and shall never be convinced that we could not have done something for him, brought him back or at least stayed and comforted him in some way while he was dying. Did he die? Perhaps he wasn't so badly hurt as John thought. (He won't tell me exactly what he saw.) Perhaps Coulter started to crawl after us but we had gone and he couldn't get any further. He might have died of exposure or neglected wounds or simply of despair that he'd been left behind. Anything. I cannot, cannot forget it.

There have been stories of men who have been lying out wounded and crying in pain and have stuffed their fists or the sleeves of their tunics in their mouths to stop themselves, knowing that they would only bring out rescue parties who would be risking their lives, for hopeless cases. The more I hear from John and the others, the more amazed I am by the astonishing bravery of many men and by their tolerance of pain and terrible conditions, *and* by the part that chance, accident and coincidence play in this war. But I wish that Coulter had died rushing towards the enemy line through a hail of fire with fixed bayonet – he was a strange, gentle man really, and yet he did have this passionate belief in the rightness of our cause and the essential evil of the whole German nation. A man after the hearts of all generals, politicians and recruiting officers. But worth the whole lot of them. He'd seen a lot of slaughter and though I abhorred all of his ideas and thought him entirely wrong-headed, yet I admired him, he was so cheerful and determined and amusing. I have written a sort of obituary, haven't I? And yet I cannot get it into my head that he is almost certainly dead. I do not *feel* it. I wish I'd seen him, no matter what state he was in. John has not mentioned him for days now but I know he feels his loss greatly and though he had no real alternative but to leave him (Oh, I do know that really, I trust John's military as well as his human judgement) yet I know he is also anxious and perhaps feels guilty, too.

There is little more to tell you for the moment. Life here changes so much and yet essentially changes very little – the daily routine is the same, the food is the same, the weather is the same, we live without a sense of time – or rather with a sense of being in army-time, which bears little relation to the time you live in. Preparations are going ahead for a manoeuvre about which I cannot tell you, we are almost off our heads with exhaustion and driven mad with orders sent along every five minutes, and with conferences every day and heaven knows what else. We are grateful for the tiny improvements in our physical conditions – life cannot have been worse than it was during those two weeks further north, we were in as bad a state as men can be. If only the rain would stop, if only I could remember what it feels like to be clean and dry.

I got your parcel, for which many thanks. I have had little time yet for appreciating the books you chose so carefully. But I have been able to retreat into other worlds once or twice – reading the Forster novel, which is so elegant and intelligent and urbane. I shall leave the rest of him up till things are a bit quieter, I like it so much. The Japanese anthology, of which I manage a paragraph every night before my eyes close (which they do too easily), is beautiful – that world seems even farther off, full of cherry blossom and reeds and still water, snow and wise thoughts. I find I can read absolutely anything (or could, if time permitted) and soak it up and it only refreshes me, whereas music has become almost impossible. We have use of the gramophone for three days out of seven now, because we have to share it with some of A Company. But of all the records you have sent, there is only the 'Winterreise' which I can bear at any time – and anything of Mozart. John is the same. Don't ask me why. I hope all the rest will not be spoilt for leave, or peace-time. Meanwhile, we know the Schubert songs by heart and each of us can always tell when the other is around by snatches of whistling.

You asked if I was very afraid of the thought of a full battle. Difficult to answer because you see I have no *real* idea of what it will be like apart from tales I have heard and from the academic tactical lectures. But I have seen enough injury and terrible death and destruction here to have no illusions about it certainly. I shall know how afraid I am when the time comes – some men say they feel only elation, others keep silent, which means they know real terror. But it is these long weeks of trench life, with the constant possibility of accident, which erodes one's courage worst of all. We have had a pep talk from the Brigadier, and last week, a pep letter came round to all officers and N.C.O.s – entirely unmoving. Yet when we were given our first marching orders at home at the end of our time in the Training Camp I felt (and we all did) a great rush of blood and glory, a singing in the ears and an eagerness to do or die. It lasted half an hour or half a day, according to how good your memory was for florid sentences!

The food here has got steadily worse and scarcer too. No idea why. God knows what they make the jam of – tree roots I think, and the stuff in the stews is obscene. We get by with the help of John's parcels, though I must say I wish that they would send less delicacies and frills and some more plain and substantial things too. Last week we had marrons glacés and crystallized pineapple.

John has just come in to say we are to go and see the C.O. yet again. Another trek and it's raining torrents, which means we shall crowd into the dugout H.Q. and sweat and steam and smell. And it won't be anything more than boring orders, more work, work, work.

'Gentlemen, I am here to tell you that we have been ordered to make a further series of reconnaissance raids up to the enemy line as far as the edge of their trenches near Barmelle Wood.'

The C.O. was looking straight ahead of him, his eyes on the patch of air, avoiding any individual face. His hands, which usually fidgeted with papers or cigar tin, were folded in front of him. He looked relaxed and curiously happy, his face was without any of its recent strain and even the skin seemed to have become smoother and taken on a more healthy look.

'There have been, as you know, five raids from B and C Companies in the past week. The information obtained from these has been negligible, through no fault of those concerned. In the course of these raids, the Battalion has lost six officers and thirteen men killed, and two officers and eleven men have been seriously wounded. In addition, B Company lost three men when in a similar raid at Leuillet a fortnight ago.'

He was silent for a moment. Barton and Hilliard sitting side by side and opposite to him in the cramped dugout, each felt the stillness of the other. Something was different, they had come for a routine briefing but the atmosphere was full of foreboding, they heard this news of the planned raids and expected that something more was to follow, the date and details of the expected offensive on Barmelle Wood.

Instead, Garrett said, 'I have made a decision and it is my duty to tell you all of the nature of that decision. I have said that in my opinion such reconnaissance raids are pointless in terms of strategy and a criminal waste of men. I have categorically refused, therefore, to pass on the orders for further raids of this sort. I will no longer accept responsibility for the fruitless loss of life which they entail. Not unexpectedly, my objections have been over-ruled. Not unexpectedly, I have been ordered to relinquish my command of this Battalion and to return to England. I expect to leave within the next two or three days. If I am wrong, I am sorry. I would ask each of you to feel entirely free to place upon record your dissent from my opinion on this matter if you wish to do so. But I cannot continue against the dictates of my conscience and my common sense, and I am entirely content that the action I am taking is the correct one.'

They realized that he had written, rehearsed and learned his speech by heart. Now that it was over he leaned back in his chair and began to look into their faces for the first time, his eyes moving quickly from one to the other, seeking some response or approval or reassurance – or hostility. He did not know what to expect. He reached for the cigar tin, opened the lid. No one spoke.

'Gentlemen, do you wish to say anything to me at all? Do you wish to ask me anything?'

Silence again.

'Then I will ask you to return to your posts and to say nothing to the men of the Battalion. Your new Commanding Officer will make whatever arrangements he thinks fit. I shall myself hope to come round the lines before I go.'

Still silent, avoiding one another's eyes, they herded out of the dugout into the teeming rain and running mud of the trench. The men glanced up apprehensively as they passed along, and their faces had the sunken-eyed look of suppressed fear. They were huddled in greatcoats and waders, trying to get what rest they could after the previous night's work of carrying up large quantities of ammunition.

'He's right,' Barton said at once when they reached their dugout. He felt suddenly faint and light-hearted from tiredness and from a sense of shock. 'He's right and he's courageous.'

Hilliard hung up his mackintosh. 'I think he just wants to be out of it all.'

'That's bloody unfair!'

'No. I think he is right about it, but I simply think that he's been half-looking for something like this, though perhaps without altogether realizing it himself. He isn't the man he was. He'd never have done something like this last spring when I first came out here.'

'Then perhaps he has just learned some sense.'

'It's the end of him, of course. His career, I mean.'

'Does that matter?'

'Would it to you?'

'No.'

Hilliard wondered whether Barton were not right after all, whether the C.O., who stood to lose most, might not simply be courageous, a man of conscience. He said, 'I've always liked him. But he's in better sympathy with you now.'

'I know.'

'And he's had Franklin for an Adjutant – that can't have made life easier.'

'Come now – Franklin is efficient.'

'I wish you weren't so bloody charitable!'

Barton smiled, turned over on his stomach, slept.

Two days later Garrett had gone. He took his leave of no one. It was the end of November.

'Is everything all right?'

'Very quiet yes.' Hilliard set down his torch. 'They'll get what sleep they can.'

'John – I'm afraid. I'm very afraid indeed.'

'Yes.' They looked at one another across the dugout. 'I'd forgotten what it was like – it seems a long time since the summer, such a lot has happened. I'd forgotten this feeling.'

'Sick.'

'That's it.'

'What about the men?'

'Oh, Fraser's gunning for victory, he's keeping them cheerful. But they don't give much away, you know how it is. Some of them are looking so tired they ought to be in hospital, let alone sent into battle.'

The near approach of the offensive on Barmelle Wood had redoubled the calls on the front line for fatigue parties, the men had worked from early morning until late afternoon, snatched two or three hours' sleep and then spent the nights bringing up ammunition and supplies.

Until early on Thursday evening the rain had continued, the whole area for miles around was a sea of mud. But yesterday it had stopped, a wind had got up, bringing a sweet stench across into their faces and flapping against the sack curtains of the dugout. Now there was a frost. For the first time their clothes had had a chance to dry out.

Hilliard said, 'We'd better turn in.'

'I shan't sleep.'

'You'll sleep.'

But Barton shook his head, reached for his greatcoat. An hour earlier Keene, the new C.O., had come down the line and the men had surveyed him, faintly suspicious, disliking changes in command. They had been loyal to Garrett – there were one or two still left who had served under him since August 1914. Colonel Keene made little impression upon them: he was a thin man, softly spoken, apparently hesitant. But a reputation for both thoroughness and toughness had preceded him to the Battalion and the required reconnaissance raids had been carried out, costing the lives of fourteen men. At the final briefing conference he had spoken concisely, had made the battle plan eminently clear to them, asked rapid questions around the table. He had, also and immediately, remembered their names.

'It seems very straightforward,' Barton had said, coming back. 'Is it likely to go off to that eminently reasonable plan of his?'

'No.'

'Are we likely to find the time schedule followed down to the last five seconds in that way?'

'No.'

'No. I thought not.'

'But to be fair, it isn't his plan, it's come from the Division and they're always like that; they're based on early cavalry manoeuvres which often did work as intended. Trench warfare is an entirely different thing, every battle since Neuve Chapelle has been some kind of mess but it will take some years until they learn about it, you see. By the next war, the message will have got through.'

'There will never be another war.'

'There will always be wars.'

'Men couldn't be so stupid, John! After all this? Isn't the only real purpose of our being here to teach them that lesson – how bloody useless and pointless the whole thing is?'

'Men are naturally stupid and they do not learn from experience.'

'You haven't much faith in humanity.'

'Collectively, no.'

'Individually?'

'Oh, yes. You've only to look around you here.'

'But you depress me.'

'I'm sorry. I haven't your naturally buoyant outlook upon the whole of life. That's why I need you around.'

'Me and Sir Thomas Browne!'

'That's right.'

'But perhaps tomorrow won't be so bad. Perhaps we really are in a stronger position than when you were here last summer. Perhaps it'll work.'

Hilliard had not replied.

'Now', he said, 'if you are going out don't be long. You really need the rest.'

'I know.'

Barton stepped out of the dugout and looked up. For the first time in weeks the sky was clear and glittering with the points of stars, a full moon shone above the ridge. The frost was thin and here and there it caught in the pale light on the barbed wire, tin canisters, helmets, and gleamed.

The night cold had taken the edge off the smell of decay and the air was sharp and metallic in Barton's nostrils. He moved quietly along the trench. In the next dugout, twenty or so men slept under greatcoats, a jumble of arms and feet. It was very still, no gunfire, no flares.

'Sir?'

'Hello, Parkin. All right?'

'All quiet, sir, yes. Funny that.'

'Hm.' Barton leaned against the side of the trench. 'You haven't been in a big show yet, have you, sir?'

'No. Have you?'

'No.'

Parkin was a year younger than himself, one of the eleven children of a cobbler – which fact occasioned three or four jokes a day about his living in a shoe. He took it with good humour, as though he were still among boys at school, entirely used to the amusement it afforded them. Jokes among the company had become either simple or obscene and childish, as the life became more exhausting and tedious.

Barton said, 'So we feel the same about tomorrow, then.'

'Do we, sir? How's that?'

'A bit queasy.'

Parkin looked relieved, nodded.

'I was thinking before you came along, sir – it's all right here at the moment. Quiet. A bit chilly but I can cope with that. There's a touch of something in the air – I don't know, maybe it's just that the bloody rain's stopped. But it's been reminding me of making bonfires and getting ready for Christmas, you know? I was feeling quite happy, just watching out and thinking. Then I got that feeling – like when you wake up and you know something a bit unpleasant's due to happen and for the time being you've forgotten what. I thought – what's up? Then I remembered.'

'I know.'

'Still – we're ready, aren't we? We've got the lot up here and we know what we've got to do. It's just a question of getting on and doing it. Maybe we'll be over there tomorrow night, they'll have run for it and we'll be kipping in Jerry's feather beds. They have everything in those trenches of theirs you know, sir – so they say, anyway. All home comforts. They dug themselves in good and proper.'

Barton watched the man's face as he talked so quickly, talked himself into some sort of reassurance, he saw the twitching at the corner of his eye, the way his mouth moved. He thought that he ought to say something to him, provide the expected words of comfort and support He could say nothing. He knew. Parkin knew.

'The left flank go off first don't they, sir? Then it's us. So we'll get the best view of the first round.'

'That's right.'

The Rifle Brigade were to take the first wave, then their own Regiment, with Highlanders in support. The C.O. had drawn the plan on a blackboard in coloured chalks, had pointed white arrows to show the direction of the artillery barrage and blue arrows to show the movement of the lines of infantry. The targets, Barmelle Wood and Queronne, were in bright green. He was a clear map maker, the pattern of it all was engraved in Barton's memory. He saw himself as a blue arrow.

'Oughtn't you to get some sleep, sir?'

Barton shifted. He was more reluctant to go in than ever, wide awake and afraid. He moved forward and looked cautiously over the parapet. No Man's Land lay, still and moonlit and beautiful.

'Yes,' he said. 'I just needed a breath of air. Goodnight Parkin.'

'Do you want to turn the lamp on?' Hilliard said.

'I thought you were asleep.'

'No, I was waiting for you. If you want to read …'

'No.'

Barton lay down, still in his greatcoat You're right "Not a mouse stirring".'

'It often happens like this, it's uncanny. I remember it in July.'

'But they must know we're up to something.'

'Oh yes. Though that fact is never obvious to High Command, whose faith in the Element of Surprise in attack is really very touching. And quite unshakeable.'

'John, shall I stop feeling so bloody afraid?'

'Things will get so busy you'll have no time for it, that's all I can promise you. But this is the worst bit, this building up of tension.'

'Like the dentist.'

'Rather a pale analogy – but yes.'

'Shall we be due for leave afterwards, do you suppose?'

'Surely. We might even get home for Christmas.'

'Both of us?'

'Anything is possible. Don't bank on it though.'

'I'd like you to come to us for Christmas but your family would object, I imagine.'

'I could come for part of the time. But really we had better not start building castles in Spain.'

'John, I want you to come and see it all.'

'Yes.'

'I want to take you everywhere, show you everything – oh, it doesn't matter if it doesn't come off for Christmas, we'll do it sometime. There's so much … I want it all to look right and be right – I want you to like them all.'

'Will they like me is much more to the point.'

'Oh, of course they will.'

'Of course?'

'Yes, because they couldn't help it and because you're my friend – and because really, they like nearly everyone.'

'So do you, don't you?'

'More or less, I suppose.'

'Has it always been like that? Has it always been so easy for you to love people? To get on with them, to bring them out, say the right things at the right time? Have you always made friends as you've done out here?'

'I've never really thought about it. But that part is easy, you know. The big outer circle of friends.'

'Is it?'

'Oh yes. It's the other which is the real luck – what we have.'

'That's another matter altogether. Things don't happen like this often in a lifetime.'

'Have you – do you have other friends who – is it the same with anyone else?'

'No.'

Hilliard felt a rush of joy and his mouth was filled up with the words he wanted to say, his head rang with them and he could say nothing.

Footsteps went by in the trench outside, voices came softly. Then silence again.

In the end they slept.

At breakfast, just after six, it was dark and still uncannily quiet. The men's faces were pale, unshaven, their eyes staring. They queued for the bread and rashers of fat bacon, stood or sat about drinking the sweet tea, and there would be nothing to do, once they were in battle order, but stand about again, watching and waiting until their turn came.

Walking along towards the Platoon Sergeant, Hilliard thought that they all knew there was very little chance of this offensive coming off as planned. In simple geographical terms the odds were against them, even though they had confidence in the strength and accuracy of their artillery. Nobody spoke much above a whisper as the dawn came up. But the sky was clear, pale as a dove's back, there had been no more rain. Between the trees of Barmelle Wood half a mile away on the ridge, a thin mist parted and for a few moments the November sun came out, so that the morning frost shone silver-white and the whole landscape seemed to spread and thin out and fade in a trick of light.

Holding the hot tin mug of tea, Barton looked up and saw it all and felt suddenly elated; his muscles were stiff from the few cold hours of sleep, he had had a nightmare for the first time since coming to France, full of images of dark green water in which he was drowning, yet now, the knot in his stomach dissolved, he was no longer afraid. He thought of Parkin a few hours before, looked along the line and remembered the hours of work that had gone into the planning of this battle, of the weight of gunpower and manpower behind them, and thought, we can do it, we can do it, Parkin was right, what is there to be afraid of? And the sun has come out, we are in luck. We must be in luck.

He had a vision of them all going over the top of the trench and running forward up the slope, hundreds and hundreds of them.

'All right?' Hilliard had come back and was standing for a moment beside him. He looked puzzled.

'Yes. I really am.' For he felt it, he had a hallucinatory sense of possessing more than one man's share of strength and confidence and hope. *It will be all right.*

'Good.'

'Look …' Barton nodded up towards the slope and the wood, to where they could just see Queronne in the lemon-white light.

'It's like a Turner canvas.'

Hilliard frowned.

'No – it is. The sun won't last but it won't rain either, and just for now it's very beautiful. Can't you see that?'

'I can see that.'

'What's the matter?'

'You.'

'No, no, I'm fine. I haven't felt like this for weeks. Don't worry about me. You must never worry about me again.'

Filled with unease, Hilliard turned away.

A few minutes later the men took up their places all along the trench. At eight, with a roar like the explosion of a volcano, the barrage began from their artillery. The men reeled with the shock of the noise after what had been such an unnaturally long silence. But then, for some time there was a sense of general excitement as they watched the smoke begin to rise up in the direction of the enemy front line, saw the great flashes of flame and fountains of earth as the guns scored direct hits.

Half an hour later the Rifle Brigade on the left flank came out and began to advance in perfect order. As far as Hilliard could see, the plain in front of the slope was filled with men, following the barrage, sweeping on without meeting any answering fire. He felt a surge of hope in spite of himself that it was going to work after all, the Surprise Element, that this would be the breakthrough, they would go up the slope and breach the wood, take over the trenches and gun positions before the Germans had recovered from the bombardment, which was now the strongest he had ever known. He looked at his watch. He wanted to go, to have it over with.

The Rifles were still advancing. They were beautiful, Barton thought, standing a dozen yards away behind Private Flannery, they are perfectly ordered, lines unbroken, graceful as horses. They are beautiful.

As the noise of the artillery got louder his excitement seemed to fill his body, took him over entirely so that, when they themselves began to go up and over the top, he was no longer conscious of anything except the urge to move forward, to keep up this almost hysterical sense of pleasure in what was so obviously a perfect battle, so easy, effortless. He felt as though he were standing outside himself, and was surprised at this new person he had become, surprised at everything. He wondered when he would come to.

Where the ground began to slope up, the mud gave way to grass here and there. But they could no longer see the men on the right and left flanks because of the denseness of the smoke. Hilliard was separated from Barton and not so far ahead, so that when the rifle and machine gun fire opened up from the enemy guns hidden in Barmelle Wood, he had a better view. He watched their own first line stagger and fall, the men going down one after another on their knees and then, before the smoke closed up, the line immediately behind. It went on like that and after a moment they themselves were caught up in it, and the heavy shells began to come over, the whole Division was an open target for the enemy guns. Wave after wave of men came walking into the fire, the ground began to open under their feet, as the howitzers blew up dozens of men at a time.

Hilliard began to try and pull his own section of the line together, as the men fell he began shouting at them to close in, before an attack of coughing from the smoke and fumes forced him to stop, gasping for breath. Four men ahead of him and O'Connor on his right went down in the same burst of machine gun fire and he wondered how it had missed him so neatly. He went on.

After that he lost touch, the men coming up behind overtook his own section and fell in the same places, so that the bodies were piling on top of one another, the shell holes were filled and then new ones opened up, filled again. Once, Hilliard slipped and fell and for a moment thought that he had been hit, but could feel no pain. A Corporal beside him was holding his head between his hands, covering his eyes and rocking silently to and fro. Hilliard crawled over, hunted for his water bottle and got a little of it between the man's lips, but as it dribbled down his throat, he coughed it up with a great spout of blood, and his head fell forward. Hilliard left him, got up again. He had no idea how far he had gone, he could see nothing. He thought they had begun to walk into their own artillery barrage, but there was a constant spray of fire from the enemy line. He had a clear picture of the whole English army caught in the neatest, simplest possible trap. Another line of men came up the slope. A Company, he thought, stepping between the already dead and wounded, walking directly on into the rain of fire, and suddenly, Hilliard wanted to stand up and wave at them, shout, push them back, he saw that it was all useless, that those few who did reach the enemy line would be shot to pieces on their wire. He turned and began to roar at the first man who came towards him but before he was near enough he fell forwards, his knees giving slowly under him and his helmet slipping over his face.

In the end Hilliard gave up and went on because, in the total confusion, it was impossible to know how else to behave. Men were rushing from shell hole to shell hole, completely out of order, trying only to avoid the fire now, and caught every so often running straight out of the way of a bullet into the face of an exploding shell. The cries of the wounded men were drowned in the din but now and again came out piercingly clear in the odd seconds of pause between blasts.

'Mr Hilliard ...'

'Parkin.'

The man was panting, scrambling to his feet. 'If you come over here sir, we can get through, there's a space. We can get into the trees.'

'Where are we?'

'To the east a bit, I think, but I haven't seen any of our own Company for ages. I came back to find someone. Captain Sparrow's dead, sir, I was going to ask him what to do – I met him, he was sitting down, I thought ...Only he was dead. Look, if we go this way.'

They seemed to have lost everyone, to be dodging only among dead bodies and great craters and mounds of turned-up mud and smoke, there might have been no other men left except those who were ahead, still firing the guns. Hilliard followed Parkin, they ducked and ran forward as they could. He wondered again how they were managing to stay alive. Then suddenly they came between the stumps of some trees, dropped down into a shell hole. Parkin scrambled out again.

'We want to be a bit farther, sir.'

'Mind we don't get on to their wire.'

'No, we're to the left of it, I think, we'll be all right in a yard or so.'

'How do you know all this?'

'Luck, sir, it's all luck.'

'You're right about that.'

'Here. In this hole.'

'We can't stick here for ever.'

'What else can we do for the time being, sir? There's nothing. We've lost touch with everyone, we don't know what's going on, do we? We've got no orders and if we had, what good would they be? It'd be hopeless trying to get back now. We'd much better sit tight and wait till dark and then have a go. This is a balls-up, sir.'

'Quite.'

'We've lost half the bloody Division.'

Hilliard leaned forward, suddenly giddy, tried to reach for his water bottle.

'You've done something to your leg, sir, look …'

'No.'

'Well, it's bleeding.'

'I'd have known. It's blood from all the wounded men we've been wading through.'

He lifted his head slowly and it felt like a dead weight.

He glanced down. A huge patch of his trousers all round the left thigh was dark with blood. He had a sense of having been in this same place, and with this same wound, before, of repeating the same bit of time over and over again. His head swam.

'I haven't got a field dressing, sir, I used it up on someone else. But I'll go and find somebody, I'll get help.'

'There isn't anybody.'

'I'll get a dressing anyway. You can have it put on and then we'll wait here till this lot dies down and I can try to get you back.'

'Can you?' It seemed unlikely. Hilliard was feeling no pain at all, only this sensation of lightness, of floating, so that his eyes would not focus and he heard Parkin's voice as from a great distance down a tunnel.

'Come on, sir.'

'What are you doing?'

'Get a bit further down in this hole, sir, you'll be better off.'

Somehow, Hilliard slithered down on his back.

'How are you off for water, sir?'

'I don't know.'

He felt the man put something to his mouth, swallowed twice, and tasted rum from his own hip flask, warm and curiously sweet trickling down the back of his throat into his belly.

'I'll be back, sir.'

He wanted to agree but as he fell further down the side of the shell hole his face came up against something cold

and soft and he felt himself sinking into a whirl of black-
ness and silence.

The first time he regained consciousness, the gunfire
was still going on all around him but it sounded now to
be mainly heavy shells. The air stank. He lay, trying to
make out where he was, for a moment, and then as he
came to, wondered what had happened to Parkin. It was
almost dark. Hadn't he been left out here some time in
the morning? He sat up and was sick into the ground at
his feet. He had been lying next to a dead man and on top
of another – or perhaps more than one. A leg had fallen
heavily across his own and when he tried to shift himself,
the first real pain he had felt shot through his leg from
the foot upwards, making him faint again. As he lost consciousness, he realized that he was thirsty. He could not
reach around to find his water bottle.

This time he dreamed, and his dream was of swimming
with Beth out beyond the point, in the bay at Hawton. The
sun glittered and shone on the wrinkled surface of the water
and he felt his body striking easily through it, felt a sense of
jubilation, as he saw her moving in front of him. But when
he caught up she turned, laughing, and it was not Beth
after all, it was David Barton and they were not children,
though the day was the same one that Beth had helped him
swim out beyond the point because he was afraid. Looking
back towards the house, he could see his father sitting in
the deckchair on the lawn, wearing a panama hat tipped
down over his eyes, hands folded in his lap, he could see the

gardener going to and fro with the lawn mower. For a long
time he swam slowly beside Barton, and then they lay on
their backs and floated, looking up at the sky, pale as paint.

'When we get back we shall have strawberries.'

'The smell of strawberries is the most beautiful smell
in the world,' Barton said and Hilliard realized that it was
true, that everything Barton said was true. He would never
forget about the smell of strawberries, now. They went on
floating and the sun shone, burning their skin, the house
and the cliffs receded.

'There's my father,' Hilliard said.

'I like him.'

'You like everyone.'

'Don't you?'

'I can't, I can't. I want to be like you but I can't.'

'Oh no, you should be quite happy as you are.'

'Why? How can I be?'

'Because it's easy.'

'But I don't like myself much.'

'Oh, you're all right, John, you're all right.' Barton was
laughing. A gull flew over their heads, silver as a bullet
they watched it land and begin to rock on the water.

'I'd like to be a gull.'

'*You are all right as you are.* listen, I know what I'm
saying.'

Hilliard heard Barton's voice in his ears sounding oddly
distorted. 'You're all right you're all right' There was something else he wanted to hear, he wanted to know the answer
to a question but he could not remember what it was. And

where was Beth? Beth had been here with them, and was no longer here, where was she? She had not liked to swim so far out and he felt suddenly afraid, because he and Barton had not looked after her, had been so absorbed in themselves. Beth was a child, she was eleven years old, she needed them to look after her, most particularly because she was plain and afraid of the water.

On the lawn his father still sat asleep in the deckchair and in the sun-filled bedroom his mother stood before the mirror, admiring herself in the lilac dress and coat. For the wedding. For the wedding.

A terrible noise burst through his head.

His leg had gone numb. He was sick again.

Now it was completely dark and quieter, except for the odd burst of a shell somewhere far in the distance. He felt better, found his flask and drank the last of the rum and then ate two biscuits from his iron ration. But there was no water left in the bottle when he found that. He wondered if he could move, to look for one that might have been beside one of the dead men. When he tried, his leg was terribly painful, but after a moment or two he found that he could get used to it. What had happened to Parkin? Why hadn't Parkin come back with the dressing? His trousers were stuck to the wound with dried blood and when he moved they began to tear away from it. He still had no idea when he had been hit. He hauled himself up on his hands, trying to get out of the shell hole, but it was raining again and the sides were slippery with mud, he could get no hold at all. His leg hurt so badly that he fell back again, his ears roared.

He came to another time to hear himself cry out and there was an answering cry. Someone had come, perhaps Parkin had returned with a dressing, or else it was some stretcher bearers. He did not mind who it was. He called out again. But after a long time, when the answering cry did not come any nearer to him, and when it sounded simultaneously with his own, he knew that it was another man wounded and crying out, probably not even hearing him. They were no help to one another. Otherwise there seemed to be no life, only death, all around him. The moon had come out for a while and he saw for the first time that he was in fact among a pile of bodies at the bottom of a shell hole, and the revulsion of it made him determine to get up and out somehow, and he found a hold by grasping the shoulders of a dead man and climbing over his back. Once up on to the level ground, he flopped on to his face, exhausted by the pain in his leg and the effort he had made. He smelled a sweet smell and the dream took him again, he was in his own room, the scent of roses came up to him from the garden.

This time it was the rain which brought him round, his head and neck were cold and running with water, his tunic was soaking wet. A Verey flare shot up and as he lifted his head he saw that he was facing out of the wood, looking down the slope in the direction of their own trenches, though they were perhaps half a mile away. He turned over slowly, his leg throbbing, found another biscuit but when he put it into his mouth, he could not swallow.

He knew now that if he was to get back it would be on his own, there would be no stretcher parties.

Above his head the moon had gone in, the sky was dark and rain-filled again and he did not want to move, he wanted to lie and drown, he could have gone back to sleep and dreamed his dreams of the sun and sea and his mother in the lilac dress, of Beth and David Barton.

Barton.

He sat up, his heart pounding. He was quite clear headed. Where was Barton? He had been further down the line and a little way behind. Hilliard had not seen him since they first went over the top. *Where was he?* He had to get back, he had to see him.

He got to his knees and tried to stand. Toppled over again at once. In the end he began to crawl, resting and then dragging himself forward, putting his whole weight on his arms, resting again. Several times he lost consciousness, he did not know for how long. From somewhere a shout. He shouted back. Nothing.

He said, 'Barton.'

He was panting with the effort of trying to go more quickly, he was forced to stop and rest for a long time. But he was out of the wood now and going inch by inch through the mud. Every couple of feet he came up against a body or a pile of bodies, odd limbs or rifles, helmets, packs. A full water-bottle. He ripped the cap off and poured the contents down his throat, crying with the relief it gave him. The next few yards were better, he could get on to his knees for a short way.

Until he came upon Parkin. He did not see who it was until the man's face was almost under his hand. He was lying on his back, arms stretched out wide and his chest and stomach half torn away. But his face was relaxed, his eyes open and looking up into the night sky, the rain splashed down gently on to him. Hilliard touched his flesh. It was cold, moist. He wondered why Parkin had come so far and whether he had been on his way back with the dressing. But looking behind him he saw that in fact he had only come a few yards out of the wood, it had taken perhaps two or three hours and felt like fifteen miles. He lay down, putting his face against Parkin's arm, and wept with frustration. Somewhere close by another man was groaning. Hilliard said, 'Shut up, shut up, for God's sake shut up!' But it was only a whisper. He felt helpless. He let his face fall forward again.

The next time he moved, remembering that he had to get back to the dugout to find Barton, the whole of his left leg and part of his side had gone numb, so that crawling was easier, though he did it clumsily. The shells were bursting around him again now but they seemed to have nothing to do with him, and he went on. He only wished there were some other sign of life apart from the crying of the wounded and the blasting of the guns.

It was not until the middle of the following morning that he reached their trenches. As he staggered forward and then tumbled down the firestep, almost knocking over a sentry, he saw that he was nowhere near his own end of the front line, the men who came along were strangers. It seemed to matter, he wanted to get up and go on, to leave them, find his own platoon. Find Barton. He heard them calling for stretcher bearers.

'You'll be all right.' Who was saying that? A man with a large nose, bending over him. 'You'll be all right.'

But it should have been Barton. Where was Barton? Vividly, then, he remembered the first time he had seen him, as he had climbed up the ladder to the apple loft at Percelle, and the sense of that place was so great, he thought that the smell of the old, sweet apples was in his nostrils and he wondered if he were not still there.

Someone put water to his lips but as he was drinking it, he wanted to get up again, he tried to sit and resented the hands of the men who were pushing him back.

'It's only my leg.'

'Yes, sir. You'll be all right now.'

He was crying, his body ached all over, his head was throbbing.

'They keep coming in like this. We had another half an hour ago but he died as soon as he got here. How do they do it?'

'How did he get here? B Company lieutenant, is he?'

'They got most of the way up, as well – this one must have been near the top of the slope.'

'I didn't think there were any of them left.'

'One or two, I suppose.'

'Let's get him up, Hammond.'

'It's all right, sir, we've got you. You're all right.'

He heard their voices and saw their mouths opening and shutting and was too tired to take any of it in, he had no idea what they were talking about, forgot where he was and did not care. He felt himself lifted up and the pain in his leg was so bad that he yelled out as they bumped him, beginning to walk along the trench.

Twice they had to get into a traverse or duck down because of shells coming over and exploding nearby. Hilliard wondered how it could be worth their while to send down shells, for how many men were left alive after all those he had seen dead, on his way down here? The stretcher bearers were swearing as they lifted him up again.

'Oh Jesus Christ!'

'Sorry, sir. We'll be as steady as we can. But they keep sending stuff over.'

Hilliard was puzzled. What were they saying? Were they talking to him? Who were they talking to? What was happening? He did not know. He knew nothing.

'Hilliard.'

The voice came from somewhere else, it had nothing to do with him. And then suddenly it was near, his ears were full of it, he felt the words hitting him in the face like blows.

'Hilliard.'

He remembered someone saying, 'lift him down.'

Who was talking to him?

'Hilliard.'

He opened his eyes. Captain Franklin's face came into focus, the same blank face, behind the gingerbread moustache.

Then he remembered that people had been before, people he knew, his name had been spoken to him. Who had come? There was something he wanted to remember.

'How do you feel?'

'I don't know.' So he could speak then? 'Yes,' he said aloud. Then again, 'I don't know.' And he heard the words quite clearly, that was his own voice. He tried again. 'I'm in a hospital.'

'Yes.' That was Franklin's voice. 'The Battalion's been moved down here for a couple of days. We'll be on our way again after that. I managed to get in to see you though.'

Hilliard found difficulty in piecing together the meaning of what he was saying.

'I'm sorry you had such a knock.'

He did not know exactly what Franklin meant by that, either. He was still uncertain what had happened to him. The nights and days slid into one another like cards and were full of disconnected noises and the pain in his leg. People came and gave him food and drink and spoke to him, he saw them staring down.

Oh God, what had he to remember? What must he try to remember?

He had heard the rain, too, pattering on and on against the windows behind his bed. Rain.

'You'll be here for a week or so. They won't send you home until they think you can cope.'

'No.'

'Is there anything you want?'

Was there?

'Has your mail been getting through all right?'

He did not know. He knew nothing.

The light went pale and then dark again around Franklin's head, Hilliard tried to focus his eyes and could not. The light went very bright, then broke into millions of shiny silver pins in front of him.

After another week they let him sit up and then he read the letters which had come from his mother and father and Beth, the letters full of formal expressions of love and sympathy, behind which lay whatever they were truly feeling.

'You've got another parcel. You get a lot of parcels, don't you?'

'Yes. Would you open it for me?'

She opened it and he made her take things around the ward again, share out figs and chocolates and cigarettes. He wanted nothing at all.

'There's another letter today, too.'

He looked at the postmark and the handwriting, and did not open it.

Yesterday a letter had come from the old Major, a short letter dictated to his daughter.

We hear things are improving out there. It's a good cause. We send our regrets that you've had bad luck with your leg. We send kindest wishes for your recovery.

They had amputated his left leg though he still did not believe it, because of the continued pain.

'Could you close the window? It's raining on my pillow.'

'Oh, we can't have you getting wet!'

She stood up for a moment looking out. She had red hair. 'Will it ever stop raining?'

Now that he was feeling so much better he did not care about his leg, he cared about nothing. But he wondered whether Franklin would come back and talk to him again, tell him what he wanted to know, tell him all of it.

There was no news. He had no visitors.

They let him sit up in a chair one morning. Then he knew what he must do. The letter had been on his table for ten days. He had to open the letter. Outside it was still raining.

'Drink your soup, Mr Hilliard. You've got to eat and drink now.'

He drank his soup.

'You're going home next week.'

In the night the sound of the guns rattled the windows. Still his leg hurt him.

Dear John,

We do not know exactly where you are – whether you are in England yet or still in hospital in France. We have no news of you but we hope that you will get this letter and, when you are better, get in touch with us. We do not know, either, how much you have heard but we beg you, if you have news, whatever news it is, to write and tell us. We have only had the telegram and then a typed letter informing us that David is missing believed killed, but we have received nothing else, none of his belongings. And we had not had a letter from him either, for some time, we were becoming anxious.

We made contact with your family at Hawton, who have replied to our letter and told us that you have been wounded and have lost your leg. But the letter took a time to reach us because ours was wrongly addressed. So we are hoping that if you are *not* still in France the hospital will forward this to you.

John, we have only you to ask for news, you have been with David, and we can only talk of him to you. There is no one else. And you have been close to him, you are sure to have so much to say to us. Please write and we will either come and see you in hospital or where you are convalescing, or at home, or hope, most of all, that you may be able to come to us. Please do that if you can, we feel that we are friends and know you so well already, we should so like to have you here to stay. I cannot write more now, I am too anxious for this to reach you, and I am afraid of distressing you when you are ill.

Yours with love Miriam Barton.

But by the time he had read it another letter had come, there were two in the same handwriting, the same postmark at which he could hardly bear to look.

I am letting you know that we received a letter from a
Captain Franklin – we think he was your Adjutant? He
could tell us nothing at all about David except that he
was believed killed in the wave of men going forward
into fire at the battle of Barmelle Wood. But he wrote
very sympathetically and kindly and now we have had
forwarded to us some things of David's, mainly books
and clothing and odd personal belongings. There was
also an unfinished letter which he was writing to us
perhaps the night before the fighting. He had not dated
it. We will not send it to you for fear that it may be
lost – we still have no news of you. But if and when you
come here to us, we should like you to read it. Unless
you have already done so, for we know David shared his
letters with you.

We are still hardly able to believe in this terrible
thing, because there is no certainty. We hear stories
of men who have been reported dead and who have
walked in at their own front doors, fit and well, weeks
later, and so we cannot stop hoping against hope, just
because of this lack of final certain news. David may be
alive in a hospital somewhere?

Then, he wrote to them, because he could not do anything but tell them the truth. He half-thought of invent-
ing a story, as he had done in the past about the deaths
of other men, forming the usual, smooth phrases about
gallant deaths, killed instantly, having suffered as little as
possible. When Fawley had blown out his own brains, he

had written such a letter, none of the man's family would ever know. He thought of it.

He wrote:

I have to tell you that I do not know anything at all *any-thing,* about David, but that it is now very unlikely indeed that he will be alive. There are not often unidentified men in hospital because we all wear tags and these are almost always forwarded to the Division. I do not believe that David can be alive after having seen where he was that day. It is likely, as the Adjutant has said, that he was walking into the line of fire and was shot down. But *I do not know.*

Please do not think that I am deliberately trying to kill your hopes but it seems best to me that you should know what is the most likely truth.

I am glad that you have now his things at home with you.

I am returning to England in two days' time now, and will probably be in hospital and then convalescent near Oxford. I am out of the war for good, of course, but cannot look ahead at all. I am feeling better and learning to manage crutches.

Please, I would rather that you did not come and see me in hospital or especially, at home. I would rather wait for a while. But I should like to have a letter if you can write to me and I should like to come and see you when I am able. It will not be for some time. I want to see you in the places I have heard about. I will let you know when it can be.

No, I did not see the last letter, we were very busy for

nights before the battle, and we saw very little of one another at all, for talking or reading. There were only a few hours, the night before the battle, when we had a word, and I will tell you of that, though there is little to tell, when I do see you.

It was another hour before they finally pulled away from the harbour. The boat was not so crowded as Hilliard had expected, and he managed to find a corner and ensure some privacy by hemming himself in with cases and crutches. For, more than ever, now, he wanted to be private, set apart, he drew back from anyone who tried to come near to him. Only within himself, he was forced to think, to think. The worst of it was that he did not know. Their letter had made him realize that. He would rather have seen anything, so long as it had been certain.

Would he?

He no longer knew. He wanted to return to the past, nothing more.

After some time, he got a Corporal who was passing to help him up on to his crutches and he tried to walk down the boat to one of the seats by a porthole. Twice, he overbalanced, as the ship rolled, fell and swore. They got him up again. He knew that it was easier here than it would be when he got home. Here, everyone was wounded, men were bandaged, deformed, sick, nobody stopped to stare, everyone had themselves to think about most of all. He dreaded the eyes that would follow him, once he got back. Dreaded everything.

The sea was grey as gunmetal and heaving, under a livid sky. It was snowing and the snow was taken up and whirled about by the wind and splattered softly on to the glass.

He did not want to be back in England.

A gull came out of the greyness of sea and snow, beating its wings and skidding over the water.

He had a sudden complete picture of Barton in his mind, he could have turned and seen him standing there, could reach out a hand and touch him. He could …

The boat dipped, nose-down, into a trough of dark water, lifted again.

He would be at home for Christmas. Christmas …

He turned and began the painful journey back to where he had left his things.

At Dover the sleet blew down on an east wind into their faces. Some of the men were singing.

'Is there anything you would like us to bring for you, John? We shall be coming early next week. Is there anything you would have us send?'

'No, thank you.'

'Books? Do you have plenty to read?'

'There's a library here.'

'Well, you should take advantage of it, you should be reading, dear, there is always some diversion to be had from a good book, it will take your mind off things.'

'Yes.' Then he remembered. 'There are one or two books I should like.'

'Well of course, but tell me quickly, dear, I have to be

ready to leave at four, the Garnetts are coming to dinner.'
His mother took out the small gold notebook and the
small gold pencil.

'The collected works of Sir Thomas Browne.'

'B-R-O-W-N?'

'No, with an E at the end. And *The Turn of the Screw*
by Henry James, and a novel called *A Room with a View.*'

'Mr Forster.'

'That's right.'

'Yes, Harrods will have that, certainly.'

'Harrods will have them all.'

'Wouldn't you like something *light?* I could ask them to
find you some more novels.'

'No. That's all I want.'

'Do they feed you well enough? Shall I have Mary bake
you a plum cake?'

'They feed us very well. Don't fuss now, mother.'

'Well, it is the least I can do, to make sure you are properly cared for.'

'I am.'

'And how long before you will be home?'

'About another fortnight. But they will let me come for
Christmas Day and Boxing Day, before that.'

'I should hope so!'

He did not want to think about Christmas. Constance
Hilliard rose.

'You look very beautiful, mother. You always look very
beautiful.'

She inclined her head, smiled at him, as Royalty would

smile. She wore a dark fuchsia dress, full-skirted, and with a coat of deeper, more purplish red, a hat with purple feathers. When she walked away, the other men in the room looked up from their books and letters, watched her go.

Hilliard turned back to the window.

It was an old house, someone's mansion given over for the duration of the war, so that they sat among beautiful pictures and tapestries on beautiful chairs at beautiful tables. Down the long lawn between the beeches, a man swept up the last of the leaves. It was growing dark, the sky was full of great, scudding clouds. He knew no one here and had made no friends, he spoke as rarely as possible, so that they watched him and formed their own judgements, assumed that he was shell-shocked or unable to accept the loss of his leg. Men left, others came. Hilliard sat by the window, watching the sky and the black trees. He thought endlessly about Barton.

But when the books came he could not bear to read or even to open them, he only stared at the covers and kept them in a pile on the locker beside his bed.

He woke one morning and wondered what he was waiting for, how long it would take before he ceased to feel simply dazed, as though life were suspended for ever and had no longer anything to do with him. When would it begin?

He did not read the newspapers, he knew nothing about the war. He did not want to know.

Colonel Garrett came to see him. They had nothing to

say to one another. Hilliard sat in dread of the moment when he would mention Barton's name but when it came, it was strangely easy, Garrett spoke of him and he listened and it was all remote, they might have been talking about some other person, nothing of the truth was touched upon. But he was glad when Garrett went.

My dear John,
Thank you for your letter, which pleased us so much and we are all delighted that you are truly feeling better and managing life without so much difficulty. Though it must still be very bad – we suspect that you are being heroic!

We are so much longing to see you. What will the arrangements be? We hope you will be able to stay here for a few days or even longer. Come now, you *will*, won't you? We know you cannot have anything more pressing. You are not to think of the future at all just now, you are still convalescing and everyone is going to make sure that you are looked after and not troubled at all by anything. If you are on the train, then someone – I hope it will be Harold – will meet you at the station, which is about two miles from the house. But can you manage the train? Perhaps someone is to drive you up by motor car, in which case please let us know and we will send you a careful map, as we are rather hard to find.

Kindest regards to your family and love to you from us all. Oh, you cannot think how much we look forward to seeing you, how much this will mean to us! Or perhaps you can? Yes, I think so.

No, we have had no further news and have all accepted now that we shall not do so. It is very hard.

Take great care of yourself, John dear, and we are all longing for next week to come.

He had thought that he might not even be able to look out of the windows of the train at the countryside, for he remembered what the places would look like, he began to recognize them – a village, the name of the previous station, a particular belt of trees and then the lie of certain fields. Pheasants ran in great bevies from out of the hedge-rows and across ploughed fields as the train steamed by, their tails trailing long and copper-coloured in the evening light.

But when he did look, he felt at once happy and soothed, he was coming here, he was seeing it and all of a sudden, he leaned forward, his eyes unable to keep up with it, he wanted to take in every inch of land, every branch of every tree.

The sky here was wide and pale in the late afternoon sun which flooded down, glancing between the acres of beech trees. It was beautiful. It was exactly as David had described it.

The train pulled in to the station, he had to start getting himself up, there was the tedious business of crutches and doors and luggage. A man and a woman helped him, and then a porter came down the tiny platform.

'Excuse me – Mr Hilliard?'

Who was this? One of them? A young man, in a cap.

'Dr Barton sent me down to meet you – he's been called out with his own car. He was expected back but it was easiest for me to come down rather than risk your waiting about. I'm George Bennett – my father farms the land adjoining the Doctor's house.'

He had picked up Hilliard's case, they were walking slowly down the platform and out into the sunshine.

Hilliard said, 'David told me about you.'

'Oh yes. Yes. We've known one another since boys, of course.' He came up to the open car. 'I put the hood down. It's been warm here today – a bit too warm, bad sign for so early, but you can't help making the most of it. If it's too cold for you …'

'No. I shall like it. It's fine.'

The air smelled sweet and dry. It was very quiet here. Hilliard felt as if he were going through the pages of a book, following a map to a country he had always known.

Bennett put his things on to the back seat. He said, 'They'll all be waiting for you. Everyone's there, you know. Dick's home on leave. Had they told you?'

The car started, drove very slowly out of the station yard down a slope, turned into a lane.

'Hob Lane,' Hilliard said. George Bennett looked surprised.

'That's it.'

'Leading to Woodman's Lane.'

'You've been here before then?'

'No.' But then he thought that that was not true, he had been here, he had spent hours here with Barton, as they had talked in the apple loft and the tents and dugouts and billets, he could walk down the lane and paths for miles around. He knew it.

'No. I haven't been here before.'

The car turned up the lane and then they were driving into the sun.

'This is all my father's land, on either side of here. You can't see our farmhouse, it lies in the dip beyond the beeches there.'

The engine was grinding slowly up the hill. Then, they came out between the trees and saw the whole valley, sloping up gently to east and west. The sky was vast, darkening behind them.

'There's the house.'

Hilliard looked up, and ahead.